She could smell him—that tantalizing hint of seawater and pine soap—feel electricity crackling along her skin at his nearness. He hadn't moved away, but stood as still as she, just out of reach.

She glanced back down. Wow, he was magnificent—and obviously as interested in her as she was in him.

"I hate to rush you." He tucked a knuckle under her chin and lifted her face, his thumb rubbing across her bottom lip. "But if you're not annoyed, could you tell me what you *are*? Exactly?"

She grinned, the charge of excitement making her erogenous zones do a happy dance. She'd been looking for someone to use. And this guy had to be the perfect candidate. He was surly, intense, gorgeous and the complete antithesis of what she was looking for in a life partner. And he clearly wanted to use her as much as she wanted to use him.

What was she waiting for?

Reaching up, she looped tentative arms around his neck, stretched onto tiptoes and tried to look as if she knew what she was doing. Seduction was virgin territory for her. She'd always let the guy set the pace before—usually after several tame dates and lots of hand-holding. Which had probably been her first mistake.

Time to seize control of your sex life, Madeleine Westmore.

HEIDI RICE was born and bred—and still lives—in London, England. She has two boys who love to bicker, a wonderful husband who, luckily for everyone, has loads of patience, and a supportive and ever-growing British/French/Irish/American family. As much as Heidi adores "the Big Smoke," she also loves America, and every two years or so she and her best friend leave hubby and kids behind and *Thelma and Louise* it across the States for a couple of weeks (although they always leave out the driving-off-a-cliff bit). She's been a film buff since her early teens, and a romance junkie for almost as long. She indulged her first love by being a film reviewer for ten years. Then, two years ago, she decided to spice up her life by writing romance. Discovering the fantastic sisterhood of romance writers (both published and unpublished) in Britain and America made it a wild and wonderful journey to her first Harlequin novel, and she's looking forward to many more to come.

SURF, SEA AND A SEXY STRANGER

HEIDI RICE

~ ONE HOT FLING ~

TORONTO NEW YORK LONDON
AMSTERDAM PARIS SYDNEY HAMBURG
STOCKHOLM ATHENS TOKYO MILAN MADRID
PRAGUE WARSAW BUDAPEST AUCKLAND

Recycling programs
for this product may
not exist in your area.

ISBN-13: 978-0-373-52811-0

SURF, SEA AND A SEXY STRANGER

First North American Publication 2011

SURF, SEA AND
A SEXY STRANGER

To my boys, Joey and Luca,
because you're amazing and I love you lots.

With special thanks to Elaine
for making Maddy's beach rescue convincing.

CHAPTER ONE

'THAT guy's got to be the world's worst surfer,' Maddy Westmore murmured in disbelief as she shivered under her lifeguard's jacket. The sleeting October rain made it hard to focus but she couldn't pull her eyes away from the tall athletic figure clad in a black wetsuit about sixty metres out in the tumbling surf. She watched with guilty fascination as he squatted on his board, steadied himself, straightened.

Then she sucked in a breath as he wobbled precariously.

The poor guy had been surfing—or, rather, attempting to surf—for well over an hour, in the sort of miserable Cornish weather that had given Wildwater Bay its name back in the seventeenth century. She'd been studying him for most of that time. The methodical way he paddled out, waited for the biggest wave and then mounted his board. But he'd yet to ride a single breaker for more than a few seconds. She had to admire his perseverance, but she was beginning to question his sanity. He had to be frozen through to the bone by now and close to exhaustion—despite the muscular build displayed by his suit—and the undertow on this stretch of beach was no joke.

'I dunno,' said Luke, her fellow lifeguard, in his broad Australian accent. 'He's got good form. Gets onto the board all right.'

Maddy's breath gushed out as Bad Surfer crashed backwards off his board for what had to be the hundreth time.

'No balance, though,' Luke finished dispassionately, flipping up his collar. 'You wanna call it?' he added hopefully. 'Beach is closed in ten minutes anyway and that storm front's gonna hit any second now.'

Feeling a rush of relief as the surfer clambered back onto his board, Maddy scanned the rest of the beach in the gathering gloom. Only a couple of hardy boogie-boarders remained inside the yellow flags they'd set up to mark the lifeguarded area. Otherwise the beach was deserted. And with good reason. North Cornwall hadn't had a great summer this year, but the weather had gone rapidly downhill as winter drew near. Even the hard core surfers had called it a day hours ago. All except one. Who was giving hard core a whole new meaning.

'Sure—' she raised her voice above the gathering wind '—let's put him out of his misery.' Crossing to the lifeguard truck parked on the sand between the flags, she grabbed the loudhailer out of the cab, already anticipating the Extreme Hot Chocolate she was going to wheedle out of her boss, Phil, when she started her afternoon shift at the Wildwater Bay Café.

The booming sound of her voice as she called in the remaining boogie-boarders and the surfer whipped away on the wind, but the boarders responded instantly. Staggering out of the surf, they hurried across the acres of sand, making a beeline for the café. The pair waved and shouted a greeting as they passed—no doubt anticipating their own Extreme Hot Chocolates.

'Crikey, he's still at it.'

Hearing Luke's incredulous comment, Maddy spotted the surfer's black board with its distinctive yellow lightning stripe bobbing back out towards the main swell.

'He's nuts. He has to be,' she whispered. Either that or he had a death wish.

The storm clouds had darkened in the distance, hovering over the horizon like smoky black crows and the vicious cross wind had picked up pace, making the waves gallop and leap like bucking broncos. Even an accomplished surfer would have trouble riding swell that choppy. Mr Couldn't Keep His Balance didn't stand a chance. She raised the loudhailer back to her lips.

'The lifeguard station on this beach is now closing. We strongly advise you to leave the water immediately.'

She repeated the order twice more, but the surfer and his board kept paddling in the wrong direction.

'Maybe he can't hear us?' she said, trying not to worry.

The hailer had a special wind setting but, after the number of tumbles the guy had taken, his ears could be waterlogged.

'Let's get the flags in,' Luke said at her shoulder, rubbing his hands together. 'He's a big boy. If he wants to kill himself, we can't stop him.' Taking the loudhailer out of Maddy's numbing fingers, he slung it into the truck. 'Plus, I've got a hot date with Jack in an hour. With the promise of hot sex for dessert,' he finished, mentioning his new boyfriend of three weeks.

The surfer heaved himself up onto his board again, his movements sluggish.

Maddy dragged her gaze away. 'That's what I love about you, Luke,' she said, forcing the niggling concern down. Suicidal surfers were not her problem. 'You're such a romantic.'

Luke chuckled as he rolled up the flag nearest the truck. 'Hey, hot sex is romantic, if you do it right.'

Maddy lifted the base of the flag and helped Luke to heave it into the back of the truck. 'Is it really?' She gave a half-laugh, unable to disguise the wistful tone.

After a year spent rehabbing her granny's cottage, plus the lifeguarding and waitressing shifts all summer at the Bay, and most evenings given over to creating her silk paintings, she hadn't had time for romance. And she was pretty sure she'd never had hot sex. Did luke-warm count?

Maddy frowned as they wrestled the second flag into the truck together. The wind sliced through her jacket and made her nipples pebble in reflex.

Come to think of it, it was probably a miracle her bits hadn't dried up and died from lack of use. Or maybe they had. How would she know?

After Steve had stormed out last summer, accusing her of being more interested in her silk designs than she'd ever been in him, she hadn't quite been able to deny it.

Even after spending every spare hour in her makeshift studio, the silk work hadn't required nearly as much maintenance as Steve. And, okay, maybe it couldn't give her an orgasm, but it had come close when she'd completed the first of the designs inspired by the seascape at Smugglers Point—and Steve hadn't been very reliable in the orgasm department either. Which only made it all the more pathetic that she'd put up with him for so long, and agonised over their breakup for months.

She shuddered and plunged her hands into her jacket pockets, hunching against the wind. Still, at least she'd taken her brother Callum's advice for once and hadn't made the mistake of taking Steve back—or lending him the money he'd begged for, which she knew perfectly well she'd never see again.

The death of her libido and the loss of a warm body to snuggle up to at night—and wake up with in the morning—had been a small price to pay for her self-respect. Even if it hadn't felt that way at the time. She needed to stop taking in losers and strays, as Callum liked to call them, and persuading herself she could fix them. Cal might be the last person on earth to give anyone relationship advice, given that he'd never had one that lasted more than a nanosecond to her knowledge, but he'd been right about that. While their parents' never-ending marital breakdown had turned Cal into a rampant womaniser with serious commitment issues, it had turned her into Little Miss Fixit.

Steve had just been one more in a small but pitiful band of boyfriends—dating right back to Eddie Mayer, who'd kissed her at the school disco and then conned her out of her lunch money—who'd taken everything she had to give and given her nothing in return. She'd decided over the long winter months that this year she was turning over a new leaf. She had celebrated her twenty-fourth birthday two weeks ago, which meant it was way past time to stop making the same mistake over and over again.

This year there would be no more Miss Pushover. No more Miss Nice Guy. And no more Miss Fixit. This year she was going to be the one who took control and got what she wanted.

The one doing the using. Unfortunately, they were already ten months into the new year, and she'd yet to find a single candidate willing to be used.

'Hey, that's weird. Where'd he go?'

Tearing her thoughts away from her disastrous love life, Maddy noticed the sharp frown on Luke's handsome face as he stared at the horizon.

Her stomach plunged and the concern that had pawed at the back of her mind all afternoon leapt at her throat like a rabid dog.

'Did he come past us?' Luke murmured, far too nonchalantly.

Unzipping her jacket and dropping it on the wet sand, Maddy grasped the rescue board leaning against the truck.

'No, he didn't,' she shouted over her shoulder as she jogged towards the surf, frantically scanning the waves. The frigid water lapped at the ankles exposed by her full-body wetsuit as she waded into the shallows.

'I'll call it in,' Luke shouted beside her as he drew level, his own board under his arm and the coastguard walkie-talkie at his ear. 'We'll have to get the chopper out.'

'No, wait. There's his board.' She pointed, spotting the vibrant yellow flash in the turbulent waves. Her stomach hit bottom as she realised the dark shape draped across it wasn't moving. 'I've got it.'

Luke shouted something back, but the sound was lost as Maddy hurdled the incoming surf and dived cleanly into the water. The rescue board torpedoed her into the rising swell as she went under. Within seconds, the tug and pull of the tide had drained her energy and she was riding the board through the waves on autopilot. Luckily, the injured surfer wasn't too far out, the waves bearing him towards shore, but as the salt water scoured her eyes and she drew ragged breaths trying to conserve her strength, she saw him move his head. A vivid red stain stood out against his pale cheek.

He's bleeding.

She redoubled her efforts, fighting the churning water, the

distance telescoping as her arms and shoulders began to ache and her legs numbed.

Reaching him at last, she shoved the rescue board under his torso.

'I've got you; don't worry,' she yelled.

She grappled with the Velcro strap attaching his ankle to his board as a five-footer barrelled down on them. She heard a groan as blood seeped from the surfer's hairline and flowed over his sculpted cheekbone.

Concentrate. Undo the strap.

She shoved his surfboard free and wrapped her arm across him, just as the wave crashed on top of them with a deafening roar.

For a split second fear froze her as the wave sucked them down. But then the training took over. She fisted her fingers on the rescue board, her cheek pressed against his torso and kicked hard. They surfaced together, breaking back into the heaving sound and fury of the angry sea. It took Maddy a moment to orientate herself, then she paddled furiously, riding the swell as she clung to the stranger's prone body. The shore seemed a million miles away, her legs so rubbery she could barely move them, her chest screaming with the effort to draw a decent breath. She pushed the panic down and kept going.

After what seemed like several millennia, a large hand grasped her arm and hauled her upright. She squinted through the stinging salt, saw Luke's dark blond hair plastered to his head.

'It's all right; I've got him,' he yelled. 'Stand up; you can walk from here.'

Her legs shook, trembling uncontrollably as she struggled to lock her knees. How could she not have realised they were almost ashore? She hugged herself as Luke dragged the rescue board with the surfer onto the sand, then knelt beside him.

She approached in a groggy haze of exhaustion as Luke— who was much better qualified than her in pulmonary respiration techniques—examined their patient. Instead of putting the surfer in the recovery position, Luke manoeuvred him onto the waiting spinal board and fastened the Velcro strap across his chest.

'He's breathing. No need to resuscitate him.' Luke shot a quick grin over his shoulder. 'Should come round in a second. Probably took a crack on the head from his board.' Luke tilted back on his haunches. 'The paramedics can check him out properly once they arrive. Keep him strapped down just in case.' He got off his knees and stood up. 'I'll go get you both a rescue blanket to keep you warm till they get here.'

Maddy shoved the straggles of hair out of her eyes as Luke strolled off towards the truck. Despite the thump of panic still closing her throat and the brutal sting of salt in her eyes, heat coiled low in her belly as she stared down at the man she'd saved.

She tilted her head to one side, transfixed.

Maybe he wasn't classically handsome like Luke, but the dramatic slash of dark brows, high hollow cheekbones and the rough stubble accentuating a strong jaw gave him a raw pagan beauty that had Maddy's breath catching. Her gaze wandered down. Broad shoulders, a perfectly defined six-pack and long, leanly muscled flanks were exquisitely showcased by the sleek black wetsuit. The heat coiled tighter.

She shuddered, although she didn't feel remotely chilled any more, and noticed the faint blue tinge around his sensual lips. A deep moan rumbled up his chest and he moved, straining against the strap.

Maddy jerked. What was she doing? Ogling him as if he were a stripper at a hen party. The poor guy was hurt and probably freezing to death. She dropped to her knees, placed her hand against his cheek. Rough stubble abraided her palm and sent another inappropriate jolt of heat through her. She ignored it.

'It's okay,' she said, the words coming out on a breathy whisper. Mortified, she paused. Boy, did she need to kick-start her love life again if she was now lusting after strangers—and unconscious ones at that.

'You're okay. Don't move,' she murmured, touching his

forehead to brush back the thick, wavy locks falling over his brow. The blood that had been gushing in the sea had slowed to a sluggish crawl, seeping out of a narrow gash below his hairline.

She pressed her thumb to it and his eyes snapped open. Her pulse pummelled her neck as she stared into the bluest eyes she'd ever seen. The brilliant turquoise of his irises contrasted with the bloodshot whites, and looked so pure and dazzling it reminded her of an old fifties postcard of the Caribbean Sea, the colour too rich to be real.

His brow creased as he tried to rise and came to a jerking halt, his body confined by the strap.

'What the…?' The expletive came out on a gruff whisper. 'Who tied me down?'

She placed her palm on his upper arm, hoping to reassure him. Unfortunately, the feel of the rock-hard bicep bunching under her fingertips had the opposite effect on her. 'I did,' she blurted out. 'It's for your own good.'

The magnificent blue eyes narrowed. 'Who the hell are you?'

Her skin flushed hot despite the chill and the spitting drizzle of autumn rain. 'I'm one of the lifeguards on Wildwater Bay. We had to bring you in. You hit your head.'

He stopped struggling and dropped his head back, huffed out a breath. 'Fantastic,' he murmured. Bitterness clouded his eyes but it didn't seem to be directed at her. 'Thanks.' The curt word lacked conviction. 'Now, undo the strap.'

She tried not to let the commanding tone annoy her. Rudeness was probably to be expected after what he'd been through. 'I'm not going to do that,' she said in her best firm but fair Florence Nightingale voice. 'You have to stay put until the paramedics get here.'

His jaw hardened. 'No paramedics,' he said. 'Now, let me up.'

'I really don't think that's a good idea,' she replied, still channelling Florence.

'Fine; I'll do it myself.'

She watched, astonished, as he tilted his shoulder down, twisted his torso and then ripped the strap free with one hand. She moved out of the way as he struggled onto his elbows and sat up. He groaned and touched his forehead.

'That serves you right.' Forget Florence. Nurse Ratchet suddenly seemed more appropriate. 'You need to lie down and wait for the paramedics to check you out.'

He swore softly and brought his fingers away. Barely glancing at the bright red stain, he fixed chilly eyes on her. Seeing the headache in them, she bit back the rest of the retort.

He leaned forward, obviously intending to stand up.

She gripped his arm. 'The paramedics will be here any minute. You need to stay put.'

He glanced at her fingers and she pulled her hand back instinctively.

'I decide what I need,' he said, his voice rough.

Maddy fought for composure. Why was he being so flipping difficult? 'But you may have injuries you're not aware of.' His gaze drifted disconcertingly to her chest and her nipples chose that precise moment to thrust against her suit like torpedoes.

'I'll risk it.' Sarcasm edged the words as his eyes lifted to her face, but his lips twitched, almost as if he were struggling not to smile and his eyes didn't look nearly as chilly any more.

Warmth spread up Maddy's neck. Unbelievable. Was the world's worst patient coming on to her? But then he flinched and she was sure she must have imagined it.

'Hey, mate, where are you off to?' Luke interrupted the charged silence, his arms laden with the silver body-warming blankets. Maddy wondered if he'd been to Timbuktu and back to get them.

'I'm leaving.' The surfer struggled onto his feet.

He staggered and Luke steadied him. 'D'you think that's wise? You took quite a tumble.'

The man sent Luke a cold stare. 'I know.'

Maddy bristled at his rudeness, but Luke seemed unperturbed. 'At least take a blanket, fella,' he said, handing over one of the silver sheets. 'You must be frozen.'

The stranger looked down at Luke's offering, paused and then took it. 'Thanks.' He wrapped the blanket clumsily around his shoulders, his hands trembling. Maddy somehow knew that if he hadn't been on the verge of hypothermia he would have refused.

'Where are you staying?' Luke asked carefully, as if he were speaking to a wild animal that might bite his hand off at any minute. Maddy knew how he felt.

'You need a lift anywhere?' Luke added when the man shot him a look loaded with suspicion.

For a minute the only sound was the rush of the wind and the thump of Maddy's heartbeat in her ears.

Finally the surfer shook his head, the blood running unnoticed in a small rivulet down his temple. 'I live at Trewan Manor,' he said, jerking his head towards the forbidding mansion that sat at the top of the cliffs overlooking the Bay. 'I can get there on the cliff path.'

Maddy's gaze lifted to the point, a little astonished by the news. She'd been fascinated by that huge old house ever since she'd first started working at the Bay last June, the towering gables and grey stone turrets making her think of Wuthering Heights and Manderley and Thornfield all rolled into one. She'd assumed the place was empty, her artistic nature conjuring up all sorts of fanciful stories to explain its desolate appearance.

Her gaze returned to the surfer. Given his wild good looks, the man fitted his mansion's raw Gothic beauty to a T. What a shame he had Heathcliff's temper, Maxim de Winter's arrogance and Rochester's condescension to match—all traits that made for gorgeous literary heroes, but were a nightmare to deal with in real life.

Maddy stepped forward as the stranger turned to leave. 'Hang on a minute; you can't just...'

Luke thrust his arm out to hold her back. 'Don't, Mad. He doesn't want your help.'

'But that's ridiculous; he could be seriously hurt,' she whispered frantically, not sure why it mattered to her.

'You can't rescue everyone.' Luke sent her a rueful smile,

reminding her of Cal, then wrapped the remaining blanket round her and gave her shoulders a reassuring rub. 'Let's get back to the café. The first Extreme's on me.'

Maddy fisted her hands on the blanket and nodded, but her gaze drifted back to the stranger as he walked across the sand. The silver blanket fluttered in the wind like a cape. She frowned, noticing the pronounced hitch in his stride for the first time. 'He's limping,' she murmured. 'He's hurt his leg.' Concern clutched at her throat again.

He stopped to rub his thigh, then carried on walking with a laboured, lopsided gait, his shoulders stiff and erect and oddly defensive.

'Looks like an old wound,' Luke said. 'Must be why he couldn't stay on the board.'

Concern and confusion tangled into tight little knots of irritation in Maddy's stomach. What sort of macho fool spent all afternoon attempting something he was incapable of? And nearly killed himself in the process?

'Nice butt, though,' Luke said cheekily, and Maddy's eyes dipped to the firm muscled orbs of his backside, indecently displayed by the skintight suit.

Her pulse-rate kicked up again and the coil of unwanted arousal twisted in the pit of her belly.

As much as she didn't want to, she had to admit Luke had a point.

'Unfortunately, I don't think he's your type,' she muttered.

Luke laughed. 'From the way he checked out your boobs, I'd have to agree with you.'

Ignoring Luke's comment—and the renewed flare of heat it triggered—Maddy forced herself to stop admiring the studly surfer's assets. The man might have an extremely nice bum, but he clearly had far too much testosterone for any sensible woman to handle.

She'd saved his life… And, while she hadn't expected him to thank her, exactly, he could at least have had the decency to treat her with an iota of respect.

But, as Maddy climbed into the cab and Luke drove them

across the beach to the café, her breasts tingled and heat pulsed insistently between her thighs.

She squirmed in her seat.

Terrific.

Trust her bits to come out of hibernation and do the happy dance for a guy who might as well have had a neon sign above his head saying *Women—approach at your peril.*

Ryan King cursed as he hauled his leg up one more step. He dropped his head between his shoulders, counted to ten and concentrated on keeping down the nausea churning in his gut. Not easy when his thigh was throbbing in unison with the stabbing pain at his temple and his whole body was so cold he was pretty sure he was about to lose several vital appendages to frostbite.

'You stupid idiot. This is your own fault,' he hissed. 'What the hell were you trying to prove?' He winced as the words bounced off the rock face.

Great, now you're talking to yourself too.

The mighty hadn't just fallen, they'd landed flat on their face, Rye thought grimly as he gripped his thigh in hands clumsy with the cold to force his leg up the final step. Pain shot through his knee and made the groin muscle cramp. He sucked in a breath and panted as clammy sweat mingled with the salt water, making the cut on his forehead burn.

He swore and waited for the worst of the agony to pass.

Unfortunately, that gave him way too much time to contemplate just how much of an idiot he'd been.

Spending close to two hours proving that he'd never be able to surf again and practically getting hypothermia into the bargain hadn't been the smartest thing he'd ever done. Headbutting his own board and then having to get rescued by a lifeguard—and a girl one at that—had added a nice thick layer of insult to the injury. But allowing the girl's sultry emerald eyes, her slender but surprisingly voluptuous figure to taunt him into thinking he was capable of doing more with her than simply lose his temper had to count as one of the lowest moments of his life.

Maybe not as low as those first weeks in hospital, doped up to his eyeballs, drifting in and out of agony and anchored to the bed. And maybe not as low as the day, three months later, when he'd discovered it wasn't just his leg and his ego that had been irreparably damaged by the bike accident. But right down in the toilet his life had become in the last six months, nonetheless.

He'd felt the unfamiliar throb of arousal in his groin, had barely a second to rejoice at the surging heat before cold reality had doused it—leaving him feeling angry and bitter and humiliated all over again.

After they'd finished prodding and poking him, the doctors had assured him the impotence was psychosomatic and only temporary—brought on by the physical and mental trauma he'd suffered. And he'd believed them.

Until the summer evening in his Kensington penthouse when the look of pity and disbelief on Marta's face had made the truth inescapable.

One thing was certain: if a stark naked Marta Mueller with her expensive supermodel's body and her superstar *I'm yours for the taking* act couldn't get a rise out of him, no pixie-faced, sultry-eyed girl clad in a full body wetsuit was going to manage it.

Pushing the ever present humiliation to the back of his mind, Rye stumbled forward and focused instead on getting to the house in one piece. His useless leg had seized up completely, forcing him to drag it across the rocky ground, his bare feet slipping in the mud. Each bump and slide had pain stabbing under his kneecap and tightening around his thigh like a vice. He glowered at the dark clouds, the pouring rain and cruel wind a perfect accompaniment to his black mood.

He let out a shaky sigh as his fingers grasped the heavy brass handle and he butted open the pantry door with his shoulder. As he shut out the angry weather and lumbered towards the suite of rooms he used in his grandfather's house, trailing mud and water on the marble tiles, his rough humourless chuckle echoed in the darkened hallway.

If only the old man could have seen him now. In one of the many lectures Charles King had given him as a rebellious teenager, his grandfather had warned him he would have to pay for his sins in the end. Who knew the old sod would get the last laugh from beyond the grave?

CHAPTER TWO

'PHIL, can I take the rest of my shift off?' Maddy forced the request out, determined not to prevaricate a moment longer. She walked back across the empty café. They'd had all of three customers so far this afternoon and, even though the rain had finally petered out, the storm clouds were still hovering. She could have left hours ago and she doubted Phil would have objected. 'I've got something I need to do,' she said, dumping her tray on the bar and perching on one of the bar stools.

Phil's ruddy face widened into an easy smile as he slopped out the glasses. 'Damn woman, you know I'm putty in your hands. That your every wish is my command.'

'Great, does that mean I get a pay rise?' Maddy asked, fluttering her eyelashes comically, the easy flirtation a familiar game.

She happened to know Phil only dated long, leggy airheads. And she didn't qualify in either category. Plus Phil was her boss, and sleeping with the boss was a big no-no for her—one of the many little Freudian hang-ups from her dysfunctional childhood that she'd had to learn to live with.

'As soon as you go on that date with me, we'll definitely talk about a pay rise,' Phil continued, still playing the game.

'Yeah, right.' Maddy laughed. 'Listen, I'll make up the time tomorrow, if you want. Today was my last lifeguarding shift of the season,' she finished, deciding to cut to the chase.

She didn't know how long the rain was going to hold off, or how long her resolve would hold out.

Phil glanced at the clock as he set the dirty glasses into the washer. 'No need to make up the time, Mad,' he said, as she knew he would. 'You're good for it.'

Phil might be an incorrigible flirt but he was a great employer in every other respect.

'Thanks, Phil.' Maddy climbed off the bar stool, untied her apron and pulled the pins out of her hair, shoving them in her pocket. She shook her head, allowing her short cap of chestnut curls to fall into place.

'Hey, before you go, I hear congratulations are in order,' Phil remarked. 'Luke says you pulled your first floater out this afternoon like a pro.'

'Thanks,' Maddy replied, a little abashed by Phil's praise. The incident hadn't exactly ended as well as it might, which was why her conscience had been bugging her all afternoon. 'I'm afraid the job's not quite done yet, though. We didn't do any of the standard checks on the guy. He shot off so fast.'

Phil dropped the bar rag into the sink. 'Seems to me, if he left without getting checked out that's his problem, not yours.'

'Technically, maybe.' She'd been trying all afternoon to convince herself of that fact. But her conscience wouldn't let her. 'But I should have made sure he was okay before I let him go.'

What if he had water in his lungs? Or a concussion? He could even now be unconscious on the floor of his mansion. She'd never forgive herself. Having dragged him out of the sea, she felt responsible for him. Which was ridiculous, of course—and probably just another biproduct of her Miss Fixit curse—but knowing that wasn't going to help her sleep tonight until she knew for sure he was all right.

'There's not much you can do about it now,' Phil added.

'Actually, there is.' Walking round the bar, Maddy stuffed her apron and pad in their cubby hole. 'I'm going to pay him a visit.' She knew where he lived. The tide had cut off the cliff path an hour ago, but it would take her less than twenty minutes to cycle up to his home via the coast road and put her mind at rest. She crossed to the café door and grabbed her rain poncho off the hook.

'You sure he's going to want you checking up on him?' Phil called after her.

Maddy glanced back. 'No, I'm sure he's going to hate it,' she said as she tugged the poncho over her head. 'But that's his tough luck.' She shoved open the door on a surge of righteous determination. 'He shouldn't have tried to drown himself on my watch.'

As Maddy pedalled through the gates of Trewan Manor close to an hour later, righteous determination had turned to abject misery—and her rescue mission had turned into an epic farce. What had she been thinking? The taciturn man she had come to see was probably perfectly fine and would no doubt slam the door in her face, if he even bothered to open it—and the trip home in what was threatening to be a thunderstorm of biblical proportions would probably kill her.

The journey to the house along the coast road had been a nightmare. Negotiating tarmac slicked with mud and bracken from the recent storm had been bad enough, but then her old banger of a bike had lost its chain twice and the hill climb had made thigh muscles already abused by the afternoon's sea-rescue weep in protest.

The spitting rain dripped under the collar of her waterproof as she dismounted and wheeled the bike past the high hedges edging the property. Maddy glared over her shoulder at the darkening sky behind her as she bounced the heavy bike along the rutted track and prayed the storm clouds would hold off for another half an hour. She didn't have her bike lights with her, which was going to make cycling home to her cottage on the other side of the Bay suicidal if the weather let rip.

She cursed her conscience—and her compassionate nature. Callum was right. Sometimes being a Good Samaritan sucked.

Then she walked into the house's forecourt. And her jaw went slack.

The towering Gothic edifice of Trewan Manor loomed over her, looking more like Castle Dracula than Wuthering Heights. The fanciful turrets and gables were even more dramatic and over-the-top up close, while the tall, unlit mullioned windows seemed to stare at her with unblinking disapproval. She propped the bike against one of the stone pillars flanking the entrance and shivered as she mounted the three steps to an enormous oak door, feeling like Dorothy about to enter the Wizard's lair.

After a fruitless search for the doorbell, she lifted the heavy brass knocker. The loud thump echoed away on the wind.

When the door didn't budge for what felt like the longest five minutes of Maddy's life she slammed the knocker again. Twice.

Still no answer.

Maddy stepped back, more than ready to abandon her mercy mission, when a sudden vision assailed her. Of her stranger, still clad in his wetsuit, lying unconscious and alone in the entrance hall of Phantom Manor. Tiptoeing back to the door, she bent over to peer into the letterbox. She'd come all this way; it would be stupid not to take a peek.

The brass letter flap eased open with an ominous creak. She squinted, focusing on a dark shape moving down the hall, and then light blinded her. She registered a glimpse of white towelling and then pitched forward as the door flew open.

'Who the...?' shouted a gruff voice as she did a face plant into warm flesh. Warm, hard, naked flesh that smelled enticingly of pine soap and seawater.

She scrambled back so fast the blood rushed to her head. That darkly handsome face was as dangerous to her peace of mind as she remembered it. Unfortunately, so was the scowl on it.

'You're not dead,' she blurted out.

'The lifeguard,' he murmured, his eyebrows winging up. 'No, I'm not dead. Not yet, anyway.' The scowl reappeared. 'What are you doing here?' he demanded. 'Apart from moonlighting as a peeping Tom.'

'I wasn't…' She trailed off, a guilty flush working its way up her neck as she took in his attire. All he had on was a thick towelling robe, his wavy hair slicked back from a high forehead. The angry red line on it was partially covered by a plaster. She must have disturbed him in the shower. One side of the robe gaped open to reveal mouth-watering pectoral muscles and the edge of one flat brown nipple nestled in a light sprinkling of hair. Had she just had her face nestled against that?

She gulped, trying to bring her blood pressure out of the danger zone. 'I came to see if you were okay.'

The scowl deepened. 'Why wouldn't I be?' He tightened the belt on his robe and shoved the lapel back into place, spoiling the view.

'You didn't…' She paused, swallowing again to ease her bone-dry mouth. 'You didn't stay to get checked out. You should really go to the hospital after an incident like that.'

'Is that so?'

Was he deliberately trying to make her nervous with that unsettling stare?

'Yes, actually it is.'

His eyes drifted down her figure, making her uncomfortably aware of the mud on her jeans, the shapeless poncho and her 'drowned rat' hairdo.

The penetrating blue eyes lifted back to her face. 'Did someone make you my guardian angel while I wasn't looking?' he asked dryly.

'I…' She stuttered to a halt and the blush got worse.

Well, for goodness' sake. That was just plain rude.

'Gosh, I certainly hope not…' she said, his sarcasm giving her hormones a wake-up call. The man might have the body of a Greek god—but he had the arrogance to match. 'That's a job I wouldn't wish on my worst enemy,' she said, warming to her theme. Why had she ever spent a moment worrying about this guy? The man was clearly far too annoying to let a little thing like a concussion get in the way of his foul mood. 'As you're obviously not dead—' *more's the pity* '—I'll leave you to your own delightful company. Goodbye.'

She marched down the steps, ignoring the rumble of thunder as she grappled with her bike.

She was out of here. She should never have come. He didn't need her help—and she certainly didn't need to put up with his crabby attitude. She trudged down the track, the bike bumping against her hip, and promised herself this was the very last time Miss Fixit would get the better of her.

In fact, Miss Fixit was now officially dead. And good riddance.

A bellowing clap of thunder crashed above her head. She flinched as several fat spots of rain splashed onto her chin and cheeks.

'Come back here, you little fool; you're about to get drenched.' The gruff command had her indignation returning full force.

Swiping the wet hair off her brow, she twisted round to see the stranger standing in the doorway. With his bare legs akimbo and the robe flapping around his knees, he looked as dramatic and forbidding as his house.

She glimpsed a criss-cross of angry red scars above his left kneecap and quashed a dart of sympathy.

Don't you dare feel sorry for him. That's what got you into this mess in the first place.

'Cheers, Grumpy,' she yelled through the building tempest, 'but I'd rather drown.'

He shrugged and lurched back into the shadows of the house. 'Fine. Suit yourself.' The door slammed shut with a thud which was promptly drowned out by another crash of thunder.

And good riddance to you too.

Maddy had got exactly three metres before the heavens opened in earnest, the deluge soaking through the pitiful poncho and her jeans and trainers in seconds.

And only two metres more before she realised the back tyre of her bike was deader than Miss Fixit.

CHAPTER THREE

RYE refused to feel guilty as he snapped the hall light back off and listened to the rain storm attack the house.

He hadn't asked her to come. He didn't want her help. And he wanted her damn pity even less. Maybe a good soaking would teach her to stop sticking her nose in where it wasn't wanted.

But, as he made his way back down the corridor, even the ache in his lame leg couldn't stop the stab of guilt, the image forming in his mind of those mossy-green eyes, the long lashes sprinkled with raindrops, peering up at him as the soft downy skin of her cheek connected with his bare chest.

He stopped and braced his open palm against the wall, stared at the cold marble flooring beneath his feet. A stab of conscience sliced neatly through the temper that had sustained him for months and hit the raw nerve he'd been busy ignoring beneath.

'Blast!'

When had he turned into someone he couldn't stand? Someone like his grandfather?

Self-pity was an understandable indulgence, but letting the accident turn him into the same moody, humourless misery guts who had greeted him all those years ago when he'd first arrived at Trewan Manor, a grief-stricken child, was not.

He shook his head and peered at the door, wincing as the rain pelted the small stained glass window above it.

Damn, if all the women he'd seduced and enjoyed over the years—from Clara Biggs, the Truro barmaid he'd charmed into bed the day after his sixteenth birthday, right up to Marta on the morning before his fateful trip along the A30—could have heard the mean-spirited way he'd snapped at that girl, they would never have recognised him.

Hell, he wasn't even sure he recognised himself.

He'd once adored the company of women. Their soft, scented bodies, the graceful way they moved, their endless talk about nothing, their passion for dumb things like fashion and skincare. He had even enjoyed their flashfire tempers and the hours they spent in the bathroom, or the way they made leaving the toilet seat up a national emergency.

Sex had never been the only reason he'd liked spending time with women. They'd once fascinated him.

They didn't fascinate him any more and he had no desire to spend time with them now—why torture himself?—but that didn't excuse the way he'd treated the girl.

Maybe she was a busybody, but he'd seen genuine concern in those sultry eyes. And if she had felt any pity towards him, she'd got over it pretty damn quick.

He stomped back towards the door. He'd never be the reckless, easy-going charmer he'd once been, but he could at least offer the girl shelter from the storm. He could stand her company for a half hour or so, and be civil to her. She'd pulled him out of the water. He would return the favour.

His lips formed into a tight smile. And offering to help would have the added benefit of making them quits. He hated to be indebted to anyone.

He thought of her parting comment and frowned.

If she didn't want to be saved, that was her hard luck.

He heard the sharp rap on the door as his fingers closed on the knob.

She looked cute and wet and cold, like a half-drowned Little Orphan Annie. Her teeth chattered as water dripped off her clothes and splashed into a puddle on the doorstep. He noticed the ancient bike lying in a heap as she wrestled off her waterproof and flung it on the floor.

Green fire flashed in those sexy, sultry eyes as they met his and her chin jutted out.

Okay, maybe that should be Little Terminator Annie. Looked as if her earlier strop had gone ballistic. But then his gaze snagged on the outline of her nipples through the wet fabric of her T-shirt and suddenly he wasn't thinking of Annie any more, orphaned or otherwise.

'If you say I told you so,' she snarled, 'I'll kill you myself.'

He jerked his eyes off her breasts, felt the pulse of heat in his groin and coughed, an unfamiliar tickle in his throat.

'Come in,' he said, trying for stern but not quite getting there, thanks to the tickle.

He pushed the door wide and stepped back silently to let her in.

She dripped into the hallway, stiff and forlorn, then muttered something that sounded like, 'I hate you, Miss Fixit.'

He cleared his throat, the tickle getting worse. Then the heat pulsed harder as he took in the trim curve of her backside in the clinging denims.

She swept her hair back from her face sprinkling him with droplets, and said something about her bike, but the words were drowned out by the wild buzzing in his ears and the glorious swell of heat blossoming in his abdomen.

She shot an annoyed look over her shoulder. 'Don't hold back on my account. Say it. You know you want to.'

The scowl made her look even cuter. Like a pixie having a temper tantrum. His eyes snagged on her breasts again. Make that a very sexy pixie having a temper tantrum.

'What, and risk death and dismemberment?' he said dryly. 'No, thanks.'

Her eyes widened and the scowl deepened. 'So Grumpy has a sense of humour.' She slapped a hand on one slim but shapely hip and looked even sexier. 'What a surprise it's at my expense.'

The heat surged and the tickle returned with a vengeance. He coughed, struggled to focus, as something light and airy and inexplicable bubbled up inside his chest. 'Exactly who's calling who Grumpy?' The quip came out on a strangled groan as the tickle became a tidal wave of pressure, building under his breastbone and making his ribs ache.

She drilled a finger into his chest, wet curls flopping over her brow. 'Don't you dare laugh at me.' Her foot stamped and the sopping trainer squelched. 'Or you'll really have something to be grumpy about.'

He wasn't sure if it was the preposterous threat that did it, delivered with total conviction as only an angry pixie could, or the outraged colour tinting her cheeks and making her emerald eyes sparkle with fury. But the dam cracked and then broke. A sound he barely recognised rattled out—and then wouldn't stop, reverberating against the cold empty walls. He gulped in air, clutching his sides, his ribs hurting as the unfamiliar sound got richer and deeper and more out of control, filling him with a warmth he hadn't felt in months.

Maddy gaped, her outrage replaced by utter astonishment.

Her grumpy Adonis had tears in his eyes he was laughing so hard. The sound had been rusty at first, almost painful, but he was practically bent double now, his hand braced on the wall to keep him upright. His arctic eyes were alive with mischief as the barrage of laughs finally subsided to a rumbling chuckle.

She would have been less amazed if the man had started tap dancing.

She took her hand off her hip, unable to stop the answering grin tugging at her lips. She ought to be even madder at him—given she was the butt of this particular joke—but she couldn't find her anger or her indignation anywhere.

A giggle popped out and she gave his shoulder a soft shove. 'You sod.' She smiled as his eyes met hers. He grinned, twin dimples appearing as if by magic in those chiselled cheeks.

'It's not funny,' she moaned. 'I'm soaked through.'

One last chuckle choked out. 'I noticed.'

Maddy dragged in an unsteady breath. With his face relaxed and that chilly cobalt glittering with amusement, the man's brooding male beauty became spellbinding. She crossed her arms over her chest, painfully aware of what a fright she must look.

'You must be freezing.' The grin turned to an affectionate smile. 'You want to get changed?'

His gaze dipped and she shivered, not feeling remotely cold any more.

She nodded, having somehow lost the power of speech.

He indicated the way down the hall. 'Spare bedroom's third on the left. Some of my old sweats are in the chest of drawers.' His gaze flicked down her frame. 'None of them are going to fit, but at least they're dry.'

'Thanks,' she murmured, finding her voice at last. 'I really appreciate it.'

'There's an en suite with towels and…' His deep voice trailed off and for a second she wondered if he felt as awkward as she did. His dimples, she noticed, had disappeared.

'Help yourself.' He paused again, cleared his throat. 'I'll be in the kitchen when you're ready, it's at the end of the corridor.'

'Okay.' She nodded again. Then thrust out her hand. Having threatened him with physical violence—twice—her granny, Maud, would have expected her to introduce herself.

He glanced down at her palm, but didn't take it.

'I'm Madeleine Westmore.' The words sounded deafening in the pregnant silence. She lowered her voice to a whisper. 'But my mates call me Maddy.'

He's not your mate, you ninny.

'Just in case you were wondering,' she added, her hand still hanging out there.

He brushed his palm on the towelling. 'Hello, Maddy,' he said, as long strong fingers folded over hers at last. 'Ryan King. But Rye will do.'

The heat of his palm—rough with calluses—had a jolt of electricity shimmering through her bloodstream and making her pulse dance.

She let go and stuffed tingling fingers under her arm. 'Nice to meet you, Rye,' she murmured, although *nice* didn't quite cover it.

His smile spread and her hormones joined the party.

'You have no idea, Maddy,' he said cryptically.

She jerked a thumb over her shoulder. 'I should probably head to the spare room before I flood your hallway.'

Or that super sexy grin gives me a heart attack.

He chuckled, the sound low and easy this time. 'Yeah. You probably should.'

She shuffled off in the direction he'd indicated, all her nerve-endings two-stepping in time to the deep relaxed rumble of laughter that followed her down the hall.

CHAPTER FOUR

THE spare bedroom turned out to be a large, ornately furnished mausoleum dominated by a gigantic bay window that looked onto the cliffs.

The storm raged outside, wind and rain buffeting the glass and making the room even more funereal. Maddy trembled, the draught from the window penetrating her damp clothes. Skirting a four-poster bed covered with an antique satin bedspread, she made a beeline for the bathroom.

White ceramic tiles, an elegant claw-foot tub and an inbuilt gas wall heater marked this room as another refugee from the Victorian era. Luckily, the heat spread quickly as soon as she lit the fire, making the bathroom considerably more welcoming than the bedroom next door. A couple of fluffy towels, an unopened bar of soap and a bottle of men's shampoo lay on top of a wicker laundry basket. Maddy sneezed as she stripped off her muddy clothes and stepped into the tub.

Great—nothing like a snotty nose to put the finishing touches to her uber-sexy drowned rat look.

The minute the thought entered her head, embarrassment scorched Maddy's cheeks and her hormones started two-stepping again. She blew out a breath and whipped the frayed shower curtain into place.

Oh, for goodness' sake. Get real.

Ryan King wasn't interested in her. A man that good-looking probably only dated supermodels. She hadn't turned him on—she'd made him almost crack a rib laughing. There was a difference.

And, anyway, she wasn't really interested in him, either. Except in a purely physical sense. Which was simply due to her sex-starved hormones going AWOL after a year of disuse.

However delicious Rye King might be to look at, she wasn't dumb enough to have a wild fling with a sexy stranger just to scratch an itch. Whatever her hormones might want. Especially as this particular sexy stranger had an attitude problem.

A seductive smile, a few seconds of charm and chest muscles to die for hardly made up for his Rottweiler routine beforehand.

She cranked the vintage brass shower control and listened to the plumbing gurgle and hiss. Then sighed with pleasure as the water went from frigid to steaming in a matter of seconds.

She stepped under the needle sharp spray, let it massage abused muscles—and made a pact with herself not to give Ryan King's sexy grin or phenomenal pecs another thought.

And promptly broke her pact a second later.

After the luxury of a ten-minute shower, Maddy searched the old oak chest of drawers in the bedroom for something dry to wear. In the end she had to settle for a worn LA Surf Academy sweatshirt, a pair of thick wool socks and her still slightly damp knickers. All the sweatpants were far too big to wear. Luckily, the sweatshirt fell to mid-thigh. Maddy assessed her appearance in the wardrobe mirror. As long as she didn't bend over in front of him, she could preserve her modesty.

She stared at her pale legs and the shapeless lump of her torso. If only she hadn't been wearing the full-body wetsuit all summer she'd at least have a tan. Not that there had been enough sun for her tan resistant skin to get much colour. She puffed out a disappointed breath and sucked in the scent of pine soap. The sudden reminder of being nestled against Ryan King's magnificent chest had her body aching with need and her heart crashing against her ribcage.

The pact. Remember the stupid pact.

Agitated and annoyed with herself, Maddy finger-combed her shaggy curls. She sighed as they fell back into an unruly bob.

Fabulous. She was about to spend an evening with the best-looking man she'd ever set eyes on—and she looked like an undead tomboy playing dress up. If Ryan King even noticed she was female it would be a miracle.

She frowned. Which was a good thing, of course, because she didn't want him to notice her.

Do not forget the pact.

As she made her way down the darkened corridor towards the back of the house, she tried to picture Ryan King wearing his Rottweiler look to help her keep the pact front and centre. But in the picture he looked all sexy and intense, his blue eyes gleaming with…

Face it, the pact's history.

She let out a breath as she stepped into the kitchen. He wasn't there. Good, it would give her time to stop hyperventilating and think of a more doable pact. Maybe.

She took several slow breaths and tried to ignore her throbbing breasts as she studied his kitchen. The pitter-patter of rain against the large window above the stove added yet more eerie atmosphere to the cavernous space. Even in the dingy light, the window offered another spectacular view of the cliffs. If she pushed onto tiptoe, she could see Wildwater Beach below.

She flicked the light switch, illuminating beautifully carved teak cabinets, a butler sink with an authentic wooden draining platform and what looked like an original Aga cooking range. The room felt warm and inviting, thanks to the roaring fire raging in the grate. Her feet padded against the checkerboard tiles as she walked towards the heat and dumped her wet clothes in an old wicker basket under the sink. She did a three hundred and sixty degree turn but could see no sign of a washing machine or dryer or even a dishwasher.

It also occurred to her that, apart from a bowl and cup drying on the draining board, the room was spotlessly clean and completely bare and impersonal, just like the spare room. She rubbed her hands together, chilled despite the heat.

The quaint antique decor had to date back to the eighteen hundreds and suited the gloriously Gothic old house perfectly, but when she thought of the sleek black sports car she'd passed in the driveway and her host's overpowering physique and appearance, she realised the house and its furnishings didn't suit its resident at all. It seemed strange he hadn't made any effort to personalise the space. If she'd had to guess, she would have placed him in some ultra-modern city bachelor pad filled with state-of-the-art boy toys.

Maybe he'd moved in recently? Although there were no boxes or suitcases or any of the other moving paraphernalia that had lingered for months after she'd set up home in her granny's cottage last summer. Could the house be a holiday rental? But why would he choose to rent such a huge place all to himself?

She chewed on her lip, the questions buzzing round in her head like busy little bees.

Maybe he didn't live here alone? The thought made her heartbeat stutter. Not that it mattered to her whether he lived alone or not...

She shook her head. She needed a distraction before her hormones started working overtime again. Having filled the old-fashioned steel kettle and set it on the stove's hotplate, she perched on tiptoe and began to search the overhead cabinets. With the rain still pounding against the windowpanes, it looked as if she was going to have to endure her host's company for a while longer. A hot cup of tea would help soothe jumpy nerves—and, hopefully, her overactive imagination. She hummed an old soul tune as she rifled through the tinned groceries in search of tea bags.

Rye swallowed a groan and stopped dead in the kitchen doorway. An off-key rendition of Percy Sledge's *When a Man Loves a Woman* was accompanied by the sight of his house guest, clad in one of his old sweatshirts, her firm, beautifully rounded little bottom showcased in hot pink panties as she stretched up to reach the kitchen cabinets.

His mouth went bone dry as the heat, which he had assured himself while getting dressed was a fluke and didn't signify a thing, shot straight back into his crotch.

Having found what she was looking for, the girl turned slightly and bounced down. Her breasts jiggled beneath the sweatshirt and his heart slammed into his throat.

Sweet heaven. No bra. I'm a dead man.

The mouth-watering hot pink bum disappeared under the sweatshirt but, as Rye devoured slender legs, smooth muscled calves and the glimpse of her profile revealed from behind the curtain of wild reddish-brown curls, he imagined plump naked breasts, the nipples hard and swollen, swaying into his open palms, and painful arousal marched through his system like an army charging into battle.

He bent his head, stared down at the enormous tent in his fly and had to resist the urge to throw back his head, beat his chest and howl with joy.

He was harder than granite, for the first time in six long months. He felt mightier than Superman. Ready to leap Everest in a single…

The shrill whistle of the kettle curbed the superhero fantasy. But only a little. She jumped, her breasts jiggled again, and granite became tungsten.

He watched her reach for the kettle in a daze of euphoria. Then her fingers closed over the handle and his mind engaged.

'No, don't touch…'

Too late. She yelped and snatched her hand back.

'Damn.' He crossed the room, grasped her wrist. 'Did you burn yourself?'

The shimmer of tears made her eyes glitter. 'What a twit,' she said, spots of colour hitting her cheeks. 'I can't believe I did that.'

She trembled, and small white teeth dug into her full bottom lip. He forced his gaze away, so desperate to taste her he thought he might explode.

A scarlet line marred the soft flesh at the base of her thumb. 'Ouch,' he murmured.

Get your head out of your pants, King. She's hurt.

He thrust her hand over the sink, the punches of her pulse under his thumb making him light-headed. Leaning over her to turn on the cold water tap, he strained to keep their bodies apart. She flinched and he caught a lungful of her scent. His own shampoo layered with something spicy and unbearably erotic. Sweat popped out on his brow—and the irony of the situation struck him. After six months of nothing, he finally had lift off, poised to launch into orbit at the most inappropriate moment imaginable.

The tap gurgled and the water gushed out. She jumped as it splashed onto her palm, jerked back instinctively. And her bottom pressed straight into the colossal erection.

CHAPTER FIVE

What on earth was that?

Maddy's eyes popped wide, the smarting pain in her hand forgotten as her nipples shot to attention and her erogenous zones went into meltdown.

A hissed curse brushed her earlobe as he shot back, letting go of her wrist.

Maddy stood stock-still, watching the water flow over her hand. She couldn't feel it. The skin of her palm had gone blessedly numb. Unlike her buttocks, which felt as if they'd been branded.

To paraphrase Mae West, either her host had an iron bar in his pocket or he was very pleased to see her. The knowledge both petrified and excited her... But not necessarily in that order.

With all her senses on red alert, the trickle of water and the patter of slowing rain sounded almost as deafening as the low murmur of his breathing and hers. She could smell him, that tantalising hint of seawater and pine soap, feel electricity crackling along her skin at his nearness. He hadn't moved away, but stood as still as her, just out of reach.

What the heck should she say? She turned off the tap, scared to look round and more scared not to.

'I...' she began. 'Um...' Heat prickled the hairs on the back of her neck.

Good one, Mads. That's articulate.

He cleared his throat loudly, making her jump.

'It's not what you think,' his deep voice rumbled out and her nerve-endings sizzled, before she registered the meaning.

What?

She twisted round and her gaze landed on the enormous bulge in the front of his faded jeans. As her nerve-endings short-circuited, she tried to make sense of his statement.

'I don't know what you think I'm thinking—' she raised her eyes to his face '—but, if that's not one of the biggest erections I've ever seen, I'd really like to know what it is.'

He raised his palms. 'Okay; you've got me.' His lips quirked. 'You're not annoyed?' he said, sounding relieved.

'No, I'm not annoyed,' she replied, realising she wasn't, not even slightly. 'Despite the pact.'

His brow furrowed. 'The what?'

'Never mind.' *Shut up, Mads, and focus.*

She glanced back down. Wow, he was magnificent—and obviously as interested in her as she was in him. Which meant she had two options here.

She could be a girl about this and revert to type. Tie herself up in knots about whether Rye King would make a suitable mate and run off screaming into the night. And her erogenous zones might calm down in about a decade or two.

Or she could be a guy about it. Snatch the opportunity and take what she wanted for once without worrying about the consequences. And put her erogenous zones in a very happy place indeed.

'I hate to rush you.' He tucked a knuckle under her chin and lifted her face to his. 'But if you're not annoyed—' his thumb rubbed across her bottom lip '—could you tell me what you *are*? Exactly?'

She grinned, the charge of excitement making her erogenous zones do a Snoopy dance. She'd been looking for someone to use. And this guy had to be the perfect candidate. He was surly, intense, gorgeous and the complete antithesis of what she was looking for in a life partner. And he clearly wanted to use her as much as she wanted to use him.

What was she waiting for?

Reaching up, she looped tentative arms round his neck, stretched up onto tiptoe and tried to look as if she knew what she was doing. Seduction was virgin territory for her; she'd always let the guy set the pace before, usually after several tame dates and lots of hand-holding. Which had probably been her first mistake.

Time to seize control of your sex life, Madeleine Westmore.

Then she pressed against the rigid erection, felt the leap of response. And power surged through her.

She'd never been wanton before. Never been remotely reckless. But she could see now what she'd always needed was one wild, wanton, reckless fling to shock her out of her complacency.

'Exactly?' She arched a coquettish eyebrow, loving the way his sensual lips curved into a seductive grin. 'I'm flattered, big boy. And hoping like hell you've got a condom large enough for that thing,' she murmured, shocking herself.

He threw back his head and laughed.

Running large callused palms up her sides under the sweat-shirt, he sobered. 'Maddy Westmore, I think you may be my ideal woman,' he murmured.

The little clutch at the meaningless endearment barely registered on the Richter Scale of excitement coursing through her body.

She gasped as he leant down to nuzzle her neck. His stubble abraided sensitive skin as hot lips fastened on the pulse point and his thumbs brushed swollen nipples. He devoured her lips with a hungry, seeking kiss, then pulled back and swung her up in his arms. 'Come on. Condoms are in my bedroom. Let's go try one on for size.'

He strode forward, one step, then staggered and listed to one side. She leapt down before he could drop her.

He swore viciously, bending over to grab his leg.

'I'm sorry; did I hurt you?' she asked, mortified. How could she have forgotten about his bum leg?

His cheeks flushed a dull red as he looked away, rubbing his thigh. 'No.' He bit the word out.

Glimpsing the Rottweiler again, Maddy cradled his cheek, steered his face back to her. 'Good.' His jaw tensed beneath her fingers. 'So you're still ready for a fitting?'

He straightened and gave a brittle half-laugh. 'Why the hell would you want to bed a cripple?' The tone was bitter, angry, but she could hear the unhappiness beneath.

'Because it's not your leg I'm worried about.'

His eyes narrowed but the tension gradually disappeared from his face. He huffed out another laugh, the hollowness gone. 'Good point.'

He took her hand, lifted her fingers to his lips and brushed a kiss across the knuckles. The gesture was so sweet and so unexpected, she felt herself flush.

'I don't want to disappoint you,' he said, his eyes shadowed by something she couldn't read.

She had no idea what he meant, but he sounded as if he was getting all serious on her… And it was the last thing she wanted.

This wasn't serious. It was her first and last wild, reckless, wanton fling. She didn't want to know him and he didn't have to know her. Serious was for Miss Fixit. Who was dead and buried.

'As long as you can hobble to the bedroom—' she grasped his hand in both of hers, tugged him towards the kitchen door '—believe me, you won't.' If he didn't hurry up, something dumb—like common sense—was going to get in the way of her Snoopy dance.

'Hobble?' His eyebrows lifted as he followed, the limp not nearly as prominent as the bulge in his denims. 'That's not very flattering,' he said, sounding more playful than insulted.

'If you want flattering,' she murmured, fluttering her eyelashes for all she was worth and hoping like mad she wasn't promising more than she could deliver, 'you'll have to get a move on.'

He laughed as he let her haul him out of the door.

* * *

Adrenalin and desperation surged through Rye's body as he slammed the bedroom door shut. She stood before him, her breath panting out in ragged gasps and those bright green eyes feverish with desire. He grabbed a handful of the sweatshirt, yanked her into his arms.

'I want you naked,' he murmured into her curls as his hands clasped her hips, found the soft, seductive flesh beneath.

She felt smooth and warm and perfect, her lush little body vibrating as he dragged the sweatshirt over her head and threw it away. Her full breasts swayed, mesmerising him, the nipples large and red, like ripe strawberries.

Her lips lifted but she looked wary all of a sudden—and much less sure of herself.

He cupped one full orb in his palm and bent to suckle the rigid peak.

She gave a soft little sob, sank her fingers into his hair and arched into his mouth. The scent of her, the taste assailed him and then panic struck.

He had to get inside her. Now, before he lost the erection. He couldn't wait, couldn't play, couldn't risk taking the time to pleasure her too much.

Dragging his mouth away from the feast of flesh, he tumbled her back onto the bed. Struggling with his fly, his fingers frantic, he released the mammoth erection, still gloriously hard. It took him several crucial moments more to kick off his jeans. Drag off his own T-shirt.

He looked up to see her watching him. Propped on her elbows, her mouth dropped open as she stared. The shell-shocked look on her face gave him a burst of pride. She wasn't gaping at the scars; she didn't look disgusted—she looked astonished.

She didn't know the half of it. And, hopefully, she never would.

'The condoms are in the bedside table,' he said in a strained voice. 'Can you get them?' It would take him too long to shuffle over there.

She nodded and rolled over, pulling a foil packet out as he eased onto the bed, trying not to jostle his leg.

'Do you want me to do it?' she asked, her voice shaky.

'In a minute.' He curved a hand round her waist, then hooked his fingers in the hot pink knickers.

He could give her a minute. At least.

She lifted her hips and he drew the swatch of lace down slender, toned legs. God, if only he could risk taking his time. He wanted to feast on her for an eternity. She smelled so good, looked so delicious, the dim light from the storm outside gilding her pearly-white skin and making his groin throb all the harder. But fear and panic barked in his head like angry dogs, threatening the promise of pleasure, so tantalisingly close.

He pulled her slim body clumsily beneath him, slanted his lips across hers. Her fingers dug into his shoulders, her breath coming in shallow pants as his tongue delved. He cupped her sex, felt her buck as he sank seeking fingers into tight tender flesh.

Thank God. She was ready. Hot, wet, slick with need.

He ripped the foil open with his teeth, his breath sawing as he rolled the condom on one-handed.

Pain stabbed in his leg, panic clawing at his throat as he adjusted her hips, nestled between her thighs.

Do it now. Before you lose it all again.

She gasped something, grasped his neck, but he couldn't hear her through the rush of blood in his ears, the need and desperation tightening like a fist around his heart.

He thrust deep. The surge of power, of pleasure, of triumph so intense he couldn't breathe.

The velvet flesh closed so tight around him he had to withdraw, thrust again. At last he settled deep, the blast of raw heat incredible. His hips pistoned, the pain in his leg forgotten as the orgasm, cruel, elemental, unstoppable, roared through him.

He shouted out his release and charged over the edge, his lungs bursting, the wondrous euphoria raging through him like the storm outside.

CHAPTER SIX

MADDY stared at the plaster moulding on the ceiling, her disappointment almost as huge as the heavy male body smothering her.

Was that it?

Her wild, reckless, wanton fling? What a total waste of time and effort.

Ryan King may have had the sexiest body she'd ever laid eyes on—and the biggest 'you-know what'—but he also had about as much finesse as a bulldozer.

Her eyes narrowed as the shock began to clear.

She'd asked him to slow down, tried to give him a little bit of direction. But had he listened? No, he'd just charged on regardless, using his thing like a battering ram.

Okay, he hadn't hurt her. But that was only because she'd been so turned on. The way he'd ploughed into her, he could have done her an injury.

She wriggled, winced and wedged her hand under his shoulder to give him a shove. He grunted, but hardly budged. Then the still-huge erection pulsed inside her. She groaned, the too-full ache making her more uncomfortable and annoyed by the second.

This could have been so much better, so much more. If he'd taken his time, shown a little patience and consideration for her enjoyment, her feelings. Instead of which, he was obviously one of those guys who thought having a handsome face and a larger-than-average appendage was enough. Well, it wasn't, not by a long shot. Not for her. Maybe there really were women who could spontaneously combust to order with only two seconds of foreplay, but she wasn't one of them. And she refused to feel inadequate about it.

She gave him another heftier shove and bit her lip as he rolled off her to flop onto the bed beside her.

She closed her legs, noticed the tenderness between her thighs and glared at him. With his eyes closed and a smile of blissful satisfaction on his too-handsome face, he looked like a small boy who had just devoured a whole Knickerbocker Glory in one swallow.

Unfortunately for her, it had been all Knickerbocker and very little Glory.

Resentment overwhelmed her. Swiftly followed by recrimination.

This is all your own stupid fault. What the heck were you thinking?

If only she'd actually been thinking. She'd have remembered there was a reason why you had to get to know someone before you did the wild thing with them. Never had her granny's favourite saying been truer. 'If it looks too good to be true...'

Clutching the sheet to her chin, she examined the plaster some more.

She should never have let her hormones and her dismal relationship history rob her of every last ounce of self-control—and common sense. She'd known the guy was arrogant and dominant and moody, but she'd decided to seduce him anyway.

She shuffled across the bed, her overworked muscles protesting, and resentment peaked.

Well, at least she'd learned her lesson. No more wild, wanton, reckless flings, not for a while anyway. Because she was going to be paying the price for this one for days.

She swung her feet to the floor, glanced at the rain splashing against his bedroom window and sighed. And that was without even factoring in the long walk home through a hurricane.

She shifted to get up.

'Maddy?' She twisted round at the deep rumble of his voice.

He stretched, propped one hand behind his head and reached out to stroke a finger down her arm, the self-satisfied smile still in place. 'Going somewhere?'

Fabulous. Why couldn't he have stayed in a coma so she could at least make a clean getaway? Resentment flared.

'I'm going home,' she said sharply. Did he even know how disappointing he'd been?

She tried to lift herself off the bed but his fingers circled her wrist.

'Don't go. Stay a while.'

What the heck for?

'I can't stay. I've got to get back,' she said tightly, trying to keep her resentment out of her voice. Telling him how rubbish he was in bed would only make this more personal.

'It's still raining, your clothes are soaking wet and your bike has a puncture,' he said reasonably. 'It's not a good idea.'

His thumb skimmed across her pulse point and she trembled.

'It's not that far,' she lied, snatching her hand away. She didn't want to be touched. 'I can always…'

'You didn't come,' he interrupted, shocking her into silence. 'Sorry about that.'

'Don't worry; it's not a problem,' she said, not all that convinced the apology was sincere. If he felt bad about his abysmal performance, what was with that sheepish smile?

'Really?' He chuckled, annoying her even more. 'What's with the angry eyes, then?'

She tried to dim the glare. 'I'm not angry,' she said with exaggerated patience. This was getting awkward now as well as irritating. She was stark naked under the sheet she had clutched to her bosom and her nerve-endings were still popping and fizzing at the sight of that bare chest and washboard-lean six-pack—when they ought to know better by now. 'I really have to go.'

She scanned the room for his sweatshirt. Where was the stupid thing?

He took her arm. 'Why don't you hear me out before you rush off?'

Oh, for...

'Fine.' She straightened, trapped and acutely aware of her nakedness. 'But can I have the sweatshirt first?' She didn't know what he had to say and she didn't really care. But she wasn't listening to anything in the nude. 'I think it's on your side of the bed.'

His lips curved as he released her. Scooping the sweatshirt off the floor, he lobbed it to her. She heard his heavy sigh as she pulled it on.

'So what did you want to say?' she demanded when he remained silent, his gaze heating with lazy approval.

'That I'm not usually that bad.' He scraped the hair off his brow, the smile becoming almost boyish. 'There are reasons for what happened that I won't bore you with,' he murmured, his eyes darkening to a rich cobalt. 'Let me make it up to you.'

Maddy felt the pulse of response—and cursed her idiotic hormones. He might have that sexy, intense look down pat, but talk about false advertising.

'That really isn't necessary,' she said primly. Another round like the last one would probably kill off her libido for good.

'Yes, it is.'

'Look, Mr King—' time to stop this stupid charade '—I'm not interested.'

'*Mr* King?' He sounded amused. 'Was I *that* bad?'

'Yes, actually you were.' Why sugar-coat it?

He clasped a hand to his breast in mock horror. 'You wound me, Maddy.'

'Well, now you know how it feels,' she snapped, annoyed by his teasing. What was so flipping hilarious?

He frowned, then bolted upright, the lazy smile gone. 'I didn't hurt you, did I?' The colour drained from his face. 'You were so tight, but I thought you were ready.'

She flushed, a little ashamed of herself. He looked genuinely horrified. 'No. That's not what I meant.'

'Thank God.' He scrubbed his hands down his face, then

pinned her with that sexy, intense look again and her nerve-endings sizzled some more. 'Look, how about we make a deal, Madeleine?'

She didn't like the sound of that, and she wished he'd stop saying her name in that low, intimate way. But then he took her wrist again, pressed his thumb to the pulse point—and she lost focus. 'What deal?'

'I'll sling your clothes in the machine—and, when they're done, I'll drive you home myself, if you still want to go.'

'You have a washing machine?' she asked, her curiosity getting the better of her.

'Yeah.' The lazy smile was back. 'I know this place looks like a throwback to the Stone Age, but it does have a few mod cons.'

'I see,' she said, annoyingly tempted.

His offer would be a lot nicer than having to push the bike three miles down the coast road, in a rain storm, in wet jeans. No question. But she wasn't sure about that *if*. Or the way the gentle rub of his thumb was playing havoc with her pulse.

'You promise you'll drive me home? No questions asked?'

'Absolutely,' he said. But she wasn't at all sure she could trust him. He had that damn sexy and intense thing going on again.

Or that she could trust herself. Why was her pulse doing the foxtrot?

He released her wrist and lifted her chin with his forefinger. 'Go run yourself a hot bath—and I'll put the laundry on.' Leaning up on his elbow, he gave her a quick kiss. 'Relax,' he said as she tucked her bottom lip under her teeth, far too aware of the sizzle where his lips had touched hers. 'I won't jump you again. I promise.'

'All right,' she said tentatively. Not sure how he had got the upper hand but knowing that somehow he had.

She shot off to the bathroom as he slung the sheet back to get out of the bed. The last thing she needed was a glimpse of that very nice bum naked to make her lose focus completely.

Closing the door behind her, she listened to his foot thump against the polished oak floorboards as he limped out of the room.

It was only when she was neck deep in pine-scented bubbles that she discovered his promise not to jump her left him far too much room to manoeuvre.

CHAPTER SEVEN

'WHAT are you doing?'

Rye winced at the shriek of alarm as water splashed over the rim of the tub and Maddy dunked down to her chin.

He choked back a chuckle at her horrified expression—and shut the door. The twin spots of colour on her cheeks and the tendrils of damp hair sticking to the graceful line of her neck made it hard for him to breathe as he crossed the room.

'Do you mind?' she said, outraged, her angry eyes flashing at him again.

'Not at all,' he said, unable to contain a smile as he settled on the wicker seat beside the tub and extended his stiff leg.

She glared at him. 'You promised you wouldn't jump me. Remember.'

God, but she was gorgeous. Especially when she was miffed. No wonder she'd been the one to bring him back to life. At last.

'I'm not going to jump you,' he said, tucking one of the tendrils behind her ear.

He ran the base of his thumb down her throat, satisfaction coursing through his veins when she swallowed convulsively. He'd lost a lot of things in the last six months, but she'd given him one of the most precious back and he intended to thank her, in the only way he knew how. Unfortunately, it wasn't just gratitude he was feeling at the moment.

'What exactly are you planning to do, then?' she asked, eyeing him suspiciously.

He couldn't see much of her, but imagining all that flushed, rosy flesh naked beneath the water made it hard to stick to the plan he'd worked out while loading her wet clothes into his grandfather's ancient twin tub.

Of course, if he had been a gentleman, he would have let her finish her bath in peace. But he'd never been a gentleman, and he'd never been all that patient either.

He couldn't really blame her for wanting to have nothing to do with him. He'd behaved like an utter clod earlier. Why should she believe him when he told her he could do better? He hoped a lot better. She'd hardly had the five-star treatment so far.

'I plan to seduce you.'

'Oh, for Pete's sake. Will you just forget it?'

The chuckle popped out despite his best efforts. She really did look miffed. And so damn delicious he wanted to lick her all over.

'But I can't forget it, Maddy. You gave me the most spectacular orgasm of my life.'

Her eyes widened and the spots of colour on her cheek bloomed to a vivid red. 'I did?' She sounded so astonished he wanted to hug her. A little surprised himself to realise he wasn't exaggerating. Of course the intensity of his orgasm had probably had more to do with his own situation than her, but it was still the truth.

'Not only that,' he continued, keeping his eyes fixed on her flushed face, 'but you saved my life this afternoon.' In truth, she may well have saved it twice. 'I owe you.' He trailed his finger through the water, touched the pebbled nipple peeking through the foam.

She gasped and her pupils dilated beautifully. 'You do?'

'And I'm a man who always insists on paying his debts.'

'Oh, I see.' She looked so flummoxed and so turned on, he had to bite his cheek to keep from smiling.

'The only thing is, I'm not sure I…' She hesitated. 'I want you to…' Her eyes flicked to his lap and she went redder still.

He knew what the problem was.

He had already guessed Maddy's brash seduction in the kitchen had been out of character. And that she wasn't usually that sexually demanding. The women he'd bedded in the past would have called him on his atrocious performance immediately, demanding to know what the hell had happened, but she hadn't, not at first, even though she had every right to.

While inexperience had never turned him on before, he found that enchanting mix of bravado and naivety nothing short of intoxicating. And unbearably arousing.

'Don't worry about that,' he said, knowing she had to have spotted the erection. 'This is all about you.' He'd already vowed to keep the granite slab in his pants for the rest of the night. 'And your pleasure.' He cupped the back of her head, nipped her bottom lip. 'I've had mine.'

After six solid months of enforced abstinence, it was going to be the hardest thing he'd ever had to do, but his sexual potency wasn't the only thing he'd lost six months ago. He'd learned as a fumbling teenager that great sex wasn't just about getting it up and then getting off. But, during his pity party, he'd lost sight of that too.

He wanted his sex life back. All of it.

Feasting on this beautiful woman, showing her what he was capable of… And, he suspected, what she was capable of too, would be more than enough pleasure for both of them.

Stretching past her, he lifted the sponge from its dish next to the tub, dipped it into the water. 'How about I help you bathe?' he said as he stroked the waterlogged sponge across her collarbone.

Her eyelids drifted shut and a little sigh issued from her lips. 'I suppose that would be all right,' she said, her voice thick. 'If you're sure it's not too much trouble.'

His groin tightened as he watched those ripe strawberry nipples play peek-a-boo with the bubbles. He gave a strained laugh. 'No trouble at all.'

* * *

Maddy's pulse hammered against her throat, her mind racing and her skin tingling as if she had been plugged into an electric socket. The slow strokes of the sponge, under her chin, down her neck, over the top of her breasts, took all of her attention.

What was she doing? How had he talked her into this?

She was naked in a bath tub, allowing herself to be stroked into a frenzy—and she wasn't sure why. He'd seemed sincere when he said he wouldn't expect anything. But wasn't she being a bit too much of a tease, expecting him to do this and get nothing in return? Only problem was, the offer had been so tantalising.

No man had ever offered to pleasure her without expecting anything in return. It had always been the other way round. She had planned to use him for sex originally and he had definitely used her, so maybe she was entitled to all this attention and she shouldn't feel guilty about…

'Maddy, relax.' She opened her eyes to find him watching her, a rueful smile on his face. 'Stop thinking so much.'

'How can you tell I'm thinking too much?' she asked. Could those penetrating blue eyes see right into her soul? She didn't even know this guy.

He chuckled, discarded the sponge. His large hands settled on her shoulders, strong fingers massaging tight muscles.

'You're tensing up. Relax. Enjoy. We've got all night.' His thumbs traced her collarbone then drifted under the water to circle her nipples.

She let the little moan out before she could stop herself.

'That's better,' he said, like a teacher with a particularly bright pupil. 'Are your breasts very sensitive, then?'

'Yes.' She gulped the word out, not sure she could breathe as he played with the swollen peaks. 'Aren't everyone's?'

He laughed. 'Not necessarily. Some women can come like this. Others can hardly feel it.'

Exactly how many women had he slept with? From the way his clever caresses were making her breasts ache and throb and fire shimmer down to her core, she suspected quite a few.

Maddy pushed the thought away. It would only make her feel inadequate.

Her brow furrowed. And she wasn't the one who should feel inadequate.

Tender lips touched her brow as his fingers stilled on her breasts. 'You're thinking again, Maddy.'

She opened her eyes. 'I know; I can't help it.' She angled her head, took in the long fingers cradling her bobbing breasts, felt the aching response at her core. 'I'm not used to this much attention. I feel a bit awkward.'

The minute she'd said it, she wished she could take it back.

Way to go, Mads. Why not make yourself sound like a charity case?

And, anyway, she didn't feel awkward; she felt hot and achy and dangerously out of control. But what he was doing made her feel oddly exposed too.

He took his hands off her breasts, which immediately felt the loss, and brushed her hair back from her brow. 'You know something, Maddy, I've never met a woman like you.'

He levered himself off the seat beside the tub before she could reply.

Was that a compliment or a criticism?

He took a fluffy white towel out of the cabinet and unfolded it.

Maddy's heart sank. He'd got tired of her. She'd ruined her sexual adventure already—with her stupid overthinking. She'd had her chance to be seduced and she'd blown it.

But, when he turned towards her, she could see humour and seduction smiling in his eyes. 'Out of the water, Madeleine.' He held the towel up in front of him like a bullfighter. 'I want to taste you and I can't do that while you're in the bath. Not without a snorkel.'

Fire rocketed to her core and she had to clasp her arms across her chest to stop the insistent throbbing.

He wanted to what?

The grin split his handsome features, those damn dimples

winking again. 'Damn, Maddy. Don't tell me no guy's ever tasted you before? What kind of morons have you been dating?'

She was beginning to wonder the same thing herself. Just the thought of those firm, sensual lips on certain very sensitive parts of her anatomy was making her feel dizzy.

'I...' she began.

His lips tilted some more. And she realised he was looking ever so slightly smug.

'Of course they have,' she lied smoothly, stepping out of the tub and shielding herself with her arms.

The man already had the upper hand. It was way past time she wrestled back a little control here. After all, she was supposed to be the one in charge, not him.

She dropped her arms to her sides as she let him wrap the bath sheet around her shoulders.

Stop behaving like a shy virgin. You're not. You're a strong, sexually powerful woman who is about to have the most thrilling night of her life.

He pulled the pins out of her hair, then drew the damp locks to one side and nipped the cord in her neck. She shuddered.

'Great, so you like oral sex?' The low murmured question shivered over her nape.

'I love it,' she said boldly, feeling like a lamb pretending to be a lion. And started as his arousal butted her bottom through the layers of denim and towelling.

He felt huge, bigger than she remembered.

She knew her sex life had always been fairly pedestrian. She'd only had two proper boyfriends and neither of them had been very inventive in bed—and she was beginning to realise they hadn't been particularly well-endowed either. Which was why she'd wanted a wild, reckless, wanton fling in the first place. But why did she suddenly feel like a total novice? And why was heat flooding between her thighs like lava?

He swung her round to face him, rubbed his hands down her arms and placed them on her hips to draw her close. 'Good,' he said, touching her nose. 'Because I love it too. And if you taste as delicious as you smell, we're both in for a real treat.'

Oh, dear, Maddy thought as he guided her into the bedroom.

Exactly how wild and wanton and reckless was this fling going to get?

'Please...Rye.' The strangled moan finished with a long, slow groan. 'I can't. Not again. I'll die.'

Maddy fisted her fingers into his shaggy hair as his head drifted lower. She wanted to haul him back to maintain her sanity, but instead her legs opened and her back bowed, arching her into his mouth instinctively.

Her breath panted out as he licked her belly button and probed at her core with knowing fingers to expose her to his gaze.

'You're beautiful.' The whisper of hot breath across impossibly sensitized flesh made her jump as the heat pounded remorselessly back to life.

He swirled his tongue over the inside of her thighs.

'Please.' She gasped, not sure what she was begging for any more.

She couldn't come. Not again. Surely it was a physical impossibility?

He hadn't just tasted her. He'd devoured her. Feasted on every last naked inch of her skin. He'd discovered erogeneous zones she didn't even know she had. Hell, she'd discovered ones she didn't even know existed.

She'd come so many times she'd lost count. He would let her rest for a while, the lazy stroking never stopping, and then he'd start all over again.

Her body had become one raw, pulsating nerve that had surrendered totally to his will. Her flesh a slave to the rough, insistent strokes of his tongue, the knowing caress of callused, clever fingers.

'Once more, Madeleine.' He chuckled. 'I insist.'

Then he found the hard, wet, swollen nub of her clitoris with his mouth and suckled.

Maddy sobbed, the sound elemental, desperate, as the coil of heat that had been building for an eternity ignited and burst into flames. The raging inferno seared through her body and she screamed, bucking under him, the raw pulsating nerve detonating into a mass of silvery shards that rocketed her over the edge and into the abyss.

'Madeleine, are you okay?'

Maddy drifted back to consciousness, the warm fuzzy feeling of afterglow making it difficult for her to get annoyed by the wry humour in his tone.

She gave a long, slow sigh, her limbs finally reviving. 'I'm dead,' she murmured. 'Of course I'm not okay.'

Her eyelids fluttered open and a satisfied smile curved her lips to match his. Wow, she'd never had a clue foreplay could be this amazing. And Rye King was a master at it. After the hour she'd spent in his arms she was beginning to realise her past sex life had been nothing short of pathetic.

He kissed her, the taste of her own essence on his lips unbearably erotic. 'I think you'll survive,' he said as he banded his arm around her shoulders and pulled her into his embrace.

Resting her cheek against his naked chest, she could hear the pistoning beat of his heart, smell the musty scent of fresh male sweat—and feel the bulge of his erection still pulsing through faded denim. He'd refused point-blank to get completely naked with her, insisting that the rest of the evening was for her, not him. But the guilty flush crept up her neck again anyway.

That had to be painful. He'd been hard for close to an hour. As wonderful as it had been to be the focus of his attention, and on the receiving end of all his hard work, she couldn't help feeling guilty and unbelievably selfish that he'd had no release.

Placing her palm on his chest, she moved back to peer into his face. 'Rye, are you sure you don't want me to...' the silly blush got worse '…do something for you? You've given me so much.'

He covered her hand, his pensive smile making her heart punch her chest. 'Maddy, you've given me more. Believe me.'

Tenderness blind-sided her at the enigmatic comment. What could she possibly have given him that he hadn't given her back ten-fold?

'I don't understand,' she said, suddenly desperate to probe beneath the surface. 'How could I have?'

He stiffened, drew his arm away as he sat up. 'Forget it. It's not important,' he said, his expression shutting her out.

She understood instantly, she'd been dismissed. And struggled to ignore the silly little dart of pain.

She mustn't start acting like a girl now. This was a purely sexual fling and absolutely nothing more. She wasn't supposed to feel anything for this man. Nothing outside the physical. And he clearly felt nothing for her. That had been understood when they'd jumped into bed together without a thing between them except sexual attraction.

Pulling the sheet back, he got out of bed. 'I'll go stick your stuff in the dryer,' he said, his back to her as he grabbed his T-shirt off the floor and put it on. 'How about I cook us dinner before I drive you home?'

'That would be nice. Thanks,' Maddy said, disorientated by the abrupt change in his manner despite all her careful justifications. She clutched the sheet to her chest as he left the room.

The door closed behind him—and she slumped down into the pillows.

The problem was she had absolutely no experience with this kind of relationship and she didn't know the rules. While they'd been making love…or, rather, having sex…it had been easy to concentrate on the physical and nothing else. But somehow the intimacy had crept up on her while she wasn't looking. She absolutely mustn't start reading things into this that weren't there.

Ryan King was a handsome, exciting, superbly sexy enigma. And he had to stay that way. Tonight had been about sex. Incredible sex. And nothing else. The man was clearly a veteran of one-night flings. His comprehensive knowledge of female anatomy was proof of that.

She'd just have to take her cue from him. And not let her tendency to over-emotionalise and over-think every little nuance of a relationship get in the way. Clearly, personal, probing questions were not the way to go in this situation.

But, as Maddy walked into the bathroom to wash and then scouted the bedroom for her discarded clothing, all the questions she yearned to ask Rye King about his strangely barren home, about his past, about his present—and the reasons why he'd given her so much and taken so little—crowded into her head like corn kernels popping on a hot stove.

CHAPTER EIGHT

'COULD I ask you a question?' Maddy kept her eyes on the simple meal of scrambled eggs on toast Rye had rustled up.

She heard the clink of his knife and fork and looked up to find him watching her. She tried not to fidget or feel intimidated. She'd waited a decent amount of time before giving in to her curiosity. But she simply wasn't enough of a guy to let this one go.

'Sure,' he replied, but she could hear the slight edge in his voice. 'What do you want to know?'

It was hardly a fulsome invitation. The question got caught in her throat.

Spit it out, Mads. You're entitled to ask one stupid question.

The man had been inside her, for goodness' sake. He'd licked her to orgasm. More than once. Maybe it was a girl thing, but curiosity didn't have to be bad. And, frankly, after the silence that had stretched out between them ever since she'd ventured into the kitchen to find him cooking their meal, she wasn't sure she could swallow another bite until she got at least one piece of popcorn out of her head.

'Is this your house?'

His eyebrows lifted.

'It's just…it doesn't seem to suit you,' she rushed on, feeling foolish when his forehead creased. How would she know what suited him?

'That's the question?' He gave an incredulous laugh. 'Seriously?'

'Well, yes.' Some of the tension eased out of her shoulders. 'What did you think I was going to ask?'

He leaned back in his chair, stretched his long legs out and drummed the fingers of one hand on the table. The considering look he sent her made her cheeks heat a little. Why did she feel like a particularly rare amoeba under a microscope?

'I thought you were going to ask what everyone asks,' he said.

'Which is?'

'How I got to be a cripple.'

The blunt statement threw her for a moment. Until she remembered. Her gaze flicked to his thigh. 'Oh, you mean your limp.'

He chuckled, but without bitterness. Leaning forward, he propped his elbows on the table. 'Don't you want to know how I messed up my leg?'

'Not particularly,' she said staunchly. 'It sounds like it's a sore subject.'

He barked out a laugh. 'That's one way of putting it.'

She winced, mortified, as she realised what she'd said. 'I'm sorry; I didn't mean to make fun of your injury.' She lurched up, began piling their plates. 'Why don't I wash up and get going?'

'Sit down.' His hand covered hers where it gripped the plate. 'It's okay.' His thumb stroked the back of her hand. 'You didn't offend me. I'm far too sensitive about the stupid thing, anyway.'

She sat down, sighed, letting him link his fingers with hers. 'I tend to speak before I think. Steve hated it.'

'Who's Steve?' he asked, lifting her fingers and kissing the knuckles.

'My ex.' She tugged her hand away, surprised by the thump of her heartbeat at the absent gesture.

A slow suggestive smile curved his lips as he regarded her with an unwavering gaze. 'Your ex, the moron?'

Heat stung her nape and throbbed in her nether regions as she recalled his earlier remark in the bathroom about her past boyfriends—and exactly how he had remedied the problem. 'Um…yes…that would be Steve.'

She stood, took the plates again, his husky laughter making her feel hot and achy and a little embarrassed. No-strings flings clearly took a bit of getting used to. 'I really should get going. I've got the early shift tomorrow.'

Her wild, wanton, reckless fling was over and it was way past time she went home. After everything that had happened today, it would be a miracle if she managed to fall asleep before midnight.

'When does your lifeguard shift start?' he asked as she put the plates in the sink with a clatter.

'I haven't got any more lifeguard shifts. Tomorrow's the last day of the season.'

'So what shift were you talking about?'

She switched on the hot tap, confused by his sudden desire to talk. Wasn't all this information supposed to be out of bounds? 'My waitressing shift at the beach café.'

'You work at the café? On Wildwater Bay?'

She turned, leaned against the sink. He sounded astonished. 'That's right.'

He got up and crossed to her, brushing against her to switch off the tap. 'So how many times has Phil hit on you, then?'

'You know Phil?' How strange. She'd never seen Rye in the café, she would definitely have remembered.

'Yeah, I know Phil. And exactly how much of a flirt he is.' For a second she thought she detected something a little off in his tone, but then discarded the idea. Why would he care about Phil and her?

'So, has he talked you into bed yet?' he asked.

She tensed as heat rocketed up her throat. 'No.' That wasn't just off, it was totally out of order. What right did he have to ask her a question like that? And in that accusatory tone? 'He's my boss; I would never sleep with my boss.' She stopped. Why was she justifying herself? 'Not that it's any of your business.'

She hated that she sounded so lame—and that the question had made her feel dirty.

She stepped past him. 'I'd better go.'

'Hang on a minute.' He grasped her arm, holding her in place. 'There's no need to get upset. It was a valid question.'

'No, it wasn't,' she said, tugging on her arm and getting more outraged by the second.

How could she have exposed herself to this? When they'd jumped each other this afternoon, she'd never considered he might not respect her afterwards.

He had no right to probe into her sex life, just because she'd done exactly what he'd done. She hadn't thought less of him for his actions, why should he think less of her? The double standard sucked. But far worse was the humiliation that lay just beneath. She had nothing whatsoever to feel humiliated about. She was a single consenting adult who could decide to sleep with anyone she chose. But the memory of how she'd let him bring her to orgasm—countless times—made her feel defenceless. What exactly had he been thinking while he was pleasuring her so efficiently? That she was a tart?

'Phil's an operator,' he said, as if he were being perfectly reasonable. 'And I know exactly how he operates.' His eyes flicked down her frame. 'You would be fair game.'

'This isn't about Phil,' she said, the choked feeling in her throat making it hard to speak. 'It's been nice, Mr King, but it's obviously time for me to go.'

He swore softly. 'Don't start with the Mr King again or you're going to annoy me.'

'*Really?*' she said, desperate to keep her shredded dignity intact. 'Well, that will make two of us then, won't it?' She stalked through the kitchen doorway, strode down the hallway.

'Aren't you forgetting something, Madeleine?'

She heard the arrogant tone as she wrenched open the front door.

Then spotted her bike, lying in a heap by the front steps, and stared up at the stars winking in the sky.

Drat.

She swung round, her back ramrod straight. He was leaning

against the wall, his arms crossed over his chest, observing her with mocking indulgence.

'Do you mind giving me a lift home?' she asked in a clipped voice, hoping to telegraph her disapproval.

'Not at all,' he replied, pushing away from the wall. His stiff leg did nothing to lessen the insolent way he strolled towards her.

It took ten minutes for them to wrestle the carcass of her bike into the boot of his snazzy little sports car. And twenty minutes more to make the silent drive to her granny's cottage on the other side of the Bay.

Maddy fumed every single inch of the way—and kept her eyes focused on the road ahead. She waited for an apology, but it didn't come. By the time he braked in front of the tiny one-bedroom cottage her resentment had reached fever pitch.

Sleeping with a man she didn't know had been foolhardy. But she thought she'd gone into this adventure with her eyes open. Unfortunately, they hadn't been open enough. What was supposed to have been a sexually liberating experience had turned into exactly the opposite. He'd made her feel cheap.

But what bugged her the most was that for a second it had actually mattered to her what he thought. He wasn't her friend. He was her one-night lover. But what was meant to be an anonymous fling didn't seem so anonymous any more.

She gripped the door handle. 'Thanks for the lift.' And the multiple orgasm, she wanted to add with as much sarcasm as she could muster, but figured he had an ego big enough to take it as a compliment.

His arm shot across her to grab the door handle and hold it closed. 'Calm down.'

Her head whipped round. 'I *am* calm.'

'Yeah, I noticed,' he said, the planes and angles of his face tense in the moonlight. 'I have a question for you before you go.'

She stopped struggling with the door handle. 'If it's about

my sex life, I'm not answering it.' On that she was absolutely clear. He'd humiliated her enough for one evening.

'Why won't you sleep with your boss? Did Phil do something he shouldn't have?'

The audacious question was such a shock, she answered it without thinking. 'Of course not. Phil and I are friends. I just…I would never sleep with anyone who's employing me.'

'Why not?'

'Because it's unethical. And…' she sputtered '…and incredibly tacky.'

She knew she sounded prissy. But she wasn't about to go into the sordid details of her childhood—and the real reason the thought of workplace sex made her nauseous. This conversation had already got far too personal. 'Can I go now?' she said, making it very clear it wasn't a request.

'Sure,' he said, finally letting go of the handle.

She leapt out of the car, determined not to look back.

'Goodbye, Maddy. And thanks for an incredible evening.'

The statement sounded genuine—and final—and she turned back without intending to.

He shot her a casual salute. Was that supposed to be ironic? But, as the car sped off down the road, the tail lights disappearing into the darkness, Maddy felt the brutal pulse of heat at her core and the strange little hiccup in her heartbeat. And despised herself for it.

She walked to the cottage, took the key from under the eaves of the porch entrance, determined to wipe the pointless spurt of melancholy at his departure from her consciousness. But, as she shut the door and leant back against it, glad to be back in the homely surroundings, she noticed the vacant spot in her hallway where she parked her bike. Her head dropped back against the door with an audible thud.

'Damn.'

She hadn't seen the last of Rye King after all.

* * *

Rye braked at the junction and swore. Her bike was still in the boot of the car. He shifted into reverse, looked over his shoulder. Then stopped. And swung back round.

He couldn't go back, not yet. Everything was too damn close to the surface. He'd behaved like a jerk back at the house. The mention of her former boyfriend and then Phil had made something coil in his stomach that he didn't understand. And suddenly he'd had to know whether she'd slept with his friend. He'd handled the situation badly, though. He could see that now. Accusing her when all he'd really meant to do was ask.

But why had he been so determined to know?

He rubbed his thigh, the muscles cramping, shifted back into first and accelerated.

Probably temporary insanity, brought on by extreme stress. Bringing her to orgasm, watching her come apart in his arms had been incredible—but rediscovering all the wonders of a woman's body had brought with it a painful side effect. He'd spent the whole afternoon and most of the evening hard as a rock. And he suspected he had a sleepless night ahead of him, lying in a bed still infused with her spicy exotic scent.

The desire to bury himself deep inside her had been all but unstoppable and, while he'd welcomed the pain in many ways because it signified the return of his libido, by the time she'd strolled into the kitchen and he'd listened to her putting on her freshly laundered clothes while he scrambled eggs, his control and his willpower had pretty much reached breaking point.

He hadn't been in the mood for polite conversation. So, when she'd asked him that innocuous question, he'd had to stop himself from snapping her head off. He'd been sure he knew what was coming.

When he'd re-entered London society after the accident, he'd been brutally aware of the hushed whispers when he entered a room, the furtive glances at the sight of his ruined leg. Women in particular had tiptoed around the subject of his disability, trying to make him feel better by either not referring to it or referring to it all the time.

He'd expected Maddy to be like all the rest.

But she'd surprised him again. She'd genuinely forgotten about it. Her astonished response to his snarled accusation hadn't only been refreshing, it had been a revelation. Forcing him to face the fact that, after six long months, instead of dwelling on what he had lost, maybe it was about time he started making the most of what he had. The fact that, since Maddy Westmore had stepped into his life, he now had much more than he thought, hadn't escaped him either.

But the minute that bolt had hit him, another had struck him right afterwards. He still wanted her. And he didn't know how to deal with that.

He didn't rely on other people—ever—especially women. He didn't ask for or expect anything and if they asked for anything from him in return, he usually bolted straight for the door.

He wasn't interested in anything serious. Anything long-term. And he didn't want that with Maddy either. He hated that choking, claustrophobic feeling that came with any hint of commitment. A lot of things had changed since the accident, but not that. He needed his freedom. And he always would.

But how did you ask a woman you barely knew if they would be interested in a purely sexual relationship? He'd been trying to get his head around that one when the thought of Maddy and Phil working in close proximity had sent him crashing through another barrier.

It wasn't that he cared about who Maddy had been with before him. It couldn't be. He didn't do jealousy. And he wasn't possessive with women. He expected them to be faithful for the brief time they were together, but he always wore condoms so he didn't take any interest in their sexual history.

Turning into the driveway of Trewan Manor, he eased up the handbrake, switched off the ignition and stared into the darkness.

The need to know about Maddy and Phil had to be another by-product of the accident and the trauma afterwards. His pride and his confidence had been shattered in the last six months and it would take more than one night to rebuild it.

He dug his thumb into his injured muscles to ease the painful cramp—while keying the beach café's number into the hands-free phone on the car's dash. First things first. Before he saw Maddy again and figured out a way of engineering her back into his bed, he had to address a more pressing problem.

Phil answered on the second ring.

'Phil, it's Rye.'

'How's things, stranger?' Phil's voice had the easy familiarity of long-time friendship. 'Still hiding out at Hell Hall?'

'Yeah,' Rye said drolly, not rising to the bait. 'I need to drop by the café tomorrow morning,' he continued, determined to head off yet another conversation about how he needed to get out more. 'What time's the early shift start?'

He wanted to be sure Maddy would be there.

'The breakfast service starts at nine,' Phil said.

Rye tapped the steering wheel, surprised by the little spurt of anticipation. 'Great, I'll see you at…'

'Wait a sec,' Phil cut in, suspicion sharpening his voice. 'What's the hurry, all of a sudden?'

'I've got a bike that belongs to one of your employees I need to drop off.'

'What employee?'

'Madeleine Westmore.'

'How do you know Maddy?'

'It's a long story,' Rye stated flatly, not appreciating the third degree—or the tiny tinge of guilt.

Phil swore on the other end of the line. 'Please tell me you're not treating Maddy to the Ryan King Do 'em and Dump 'em routine.'

Rye's temper sparked. He'd coined that insulting phrase fifteen years ago, when he'd been sixteen, had turbo-charged hormones and thought boasting about all the women he got into the sack made him a man. 'We're not in secondary school any more, Phil.'

'Too right we're not,' Phil interrupted forcefully. 'Leave her alone, Rye; she doesn't play those kind of games.'

'What games?' Rye demanded, something sour settling in his gut. Since when had free-wheeling Phil become the protective sort? Had Maddy lied to him about the two of them?

'You know what games,' Phil said, then sighed. 'Look, mate, she's a good friend and a great waitress. She works really hard and she got dumped on big time last year by some creep called Steve. The last thing she needs is a smooth-talking, over-sexed big shot from London using her for sport.'

Rye would have laughed at Phil's insulting assessment of him—the *over-sexed* reference being particularly ironic—if the sour something in his gut hadn't been rising up his throat like bile. 'What is this? Are you trying to stake your own claim?'

'No. It's nothing like that.' Phil sounded genuinely shocked at the accusation. 'She's not interested in me. And, even if she were, she doesn't do sex with the boss. Ever. She has a rule about it.'

'How the hell do you know that?' Rye shouted, the bile threatening to choke him.

'Because she told me,' Phil shot right back. 'She was a little drunk and we were—' He paused. 'Anyway, that's not the point. What did she say when you told her you own this place? I can't believe she would…'

'I'm not sleeping with her.' Not right this minute, anyway.

Rye ignored the tug of guilt. Maybe he should have mentioned that he owned the café, but it hadn't seemed all that relevant.

He'd inherited all the property along the Bay after the death of his grandfather ten years ago, when he'd still been travelling round the world as a surf bum living off the prize money from competitions and any instructor work he could hustle. After the funeral, he'd spent two months refurbishing the café, opening a surf hire shop next door and blowing the rest of his inheritance rehabbing the old Victorian guest house on the point and reopening it as a boutique hotel to cater to North Cornwall's young, rich and sporty summer crowd. Then he'd hired Phil to manage the café and surf shop and Tony, another of his old friends from secondary school, to manage Surf Central, and got the hell out of Cornwall for the second time in his life.

That small taste of empire-building had planted a seed, though, that had blossomed into dissatisfaction as he'd back-packed his way to Hawaii. He'd got as far as California before he'd admitted that his nomadic, shoestring existence didn't have the cachet at twenty-one that it had when he'd first run away from his grandfather's oppressive rules and regulations at seventeen. So he'd made his way back to London, remortgaged Trewan Manor, arranged a loan on the Wildwater Bay businesses and started making careful investments in similar extreme sports enterprises around the globe.

The adrenalin kick of riding the perfect wave had gradually been replaced by the more intense and sustained high of managing his fledgling business empire and watching it grow and expand.

He'd worked hard to build King Xtreme into a thriving multinational concern. And, yeah, maybe he'd played hard as well, bedding a string of beautiful women the world over and turning his Kensington penthouse into the party capital of London society during the winter months. But his sexual conquests had never been indiscriminate, or nearly as prolific as the press liked to maintain—and, while he'd had a well-earned reputation as an adrenalin junkie, he'd never used drugs or alcohol to feed the high. Maintaining his health and his fitness had been an important part of his brand. Until the accident.

So he didn't deserve Phil's scorn. Or this guilt trip.

'Maddy will find out that I own the café tomorrow.' He could sort out any hang-ups she might have about sleeping with the boss then. He didn't anticipate it being a big hurdle, though, not after the way she had responded to his touch today. And, anyhow, strictly speaking, he wasn't her boss. Phil was.

'Fine. But don't say I didn't warn you,' Phil said. 'I'll see you tomorrow. The breakfast rush is over around eleven. Come by then and I can take time out to show you the books.'

'I'll be there at nine-thirty,' he said and disconnected the call.

He wasn't waiting till eleven to see Maddy again. Plus he had no desire to see the books. He had accountants to do that sort of thing. And he trusted Phil. Implicitly.

Just not with Maddy.

CHAPTER NINE

'THIS morning's breakfast special is sweet waffles with crispy bacon and maple syrup.'

Maddy waited patiently for the elderly couple to make up their minds, then jotted down their order. Pasting on what she hoped was a perky smile, she refilled their coffee cups. 'That'll be a few minutes. Feel free to help yourself to newspapers and magazines while you wait.'

Tucking her pad away, she slipped through the swinging doors into the kitchen and pinned the only order of the morning on the board.

'That's it?' said Guy, their breakfast chef, as he whisked the tab off the board. 'I might as well have stayed in bed.'

'I wish I had.' Maddy gave the small of her back a rub and glanced at the clock. She still had five hours to go on her shift and her legs already felt like limp noodles.

Yesterday's unscheduled exercise, both in bed and out, would have been enough to knock her out. But when you factored in the restless night she'd spent while a string of X-rated erotic memories played in her head—and the three-mile hike to the café this morning—she was officially dead on her feet.

'I can see that.' Guy scanned her face as he cracked eggs into the mixer. He wiggled his eyebrows. 'Hot date, eh?'

The suggestive comment had a couple of the most lurid memories popping into her head, in full senso-vision. Guy's eagle eyes narrowed as the hot flush scorched her throat.

He laughed. 'So little Maddy finally got her mojo back last night.'

'Get lost, Guy.' She threw the words over her shoulder, his amused chuckle drowned out by the whirl of the mixer.

She slammed out of the kitchen door, only to spot her mojo standing in the café doorway. Her stride faltered as the flush burned her scalp. What was *he* doing here? And why did he have to look so gorgeous?

His bronze hair had streaks of gold she hadn't noticed last night, and fell across his brow in windblown waves as those crystal-blue eyes fixed on her face.

His eyes flicked down her figure and the flush raced into her cheeks.

'Hello, Madeleine.' The innocuous pleasantry spoken in that low husky voice had a dangerous effect on her thigh muscles.

'Hello.' She fumbled a menu from the end of the bar and directed him to a table. He'd probably just come for breakfast. No need to panic. Yet.

'I didn't come here to eat,' he said, stepping towards her.

He stood too close, that clean scent of pine forests and man making the torrid memories all the more vivid.

'So why did you come?' she said, more breathlessly than intended.

'Your bike.'

'Oh, yes. Of course.' Why did the knowledge bring with it that silly spurt of melancholy again? 'Thanks.'

'And we need to talk.'

'What about?' The question came out on a suspicious squeak. His eyes had gone that intense cobalt blue, the knowledge in them making her thighs quiver.

He stroked a thumb down the side of her neck. 'Come now, Madeleine.' Strong fingers spanned her shoulder as he bent to whisper in her ear. 'We both know you're not *that* innocent.'

'Get your hands off my waitress, King.' Phil's shout had Maddy jerking back, her thighs now liquid.

Rye raised his head, winked at her, then squared up to her boss. 'I'll put my hands where I damn well like, Trevellian.'

Just as Maddy began to panic about how she was going to referee a wrestling match between two guys who were each close to a foot taller than her, Phil laughed and punched Rye on the shoulder. 'Long time no see, Hermit Man.' The smile on Phil's face beamed.

These two didn't just know each other, Maddy realised, they cared.

Rye gave his friend a brief manly hug. 'I need to speak to Maddy,' Rye said. 'We'll use your office. Then she's taking the rest of the shift off.'

She's what?

Phil's smile faded. 'Now hang on a minute, hotshot,' he said, the affection edged with irritation. 'I told you already; Maddy's not…'

'Hey, Maddy's standing right here.'

The two of them glanced at her as if *she* were the nutty one.

'And she doesn't appreciate being talked about as if she's not.'

She poked a finger into Rye's shoulder and enjoyed the flash of surprise as he stumbled back a step.

'What do you think you're playing at? Waltzing in here as if you own the place and telling me what to do.' They'd had exactly one evening together. And he still hadn't apologised for his insulting questions at the end of it.

She wasn't Little Miss Pushover any more. The new Maddy didn't take this crap. She stood up for herself. 'You're not my boss. Phil is. So you don't get to decide when my shift ends.'

Phil tapped her on the shoulder. 'Maddy.'

'What?' She spun round, not appreciating being halted in mid-rant. With a bit more practice, she could get good at this.

Phil cleared his throat. He looked like a boy caught with his hand in the cookie jar. 'He does own the place.'

'He…? What?' The blood leached out of Maddy's face and pounded into her heart.

'He's my boss,' Phil added, no longer meeting her eye. 'Which also makes him yours.'

She turned to stare at Rye, her mouth opening and closing but no sound coming out.

Sordid memory assailed her. Her father, his face ruddy, his trousers and boxers round his ankles and his large hands fastened to the plump young secretary's naked hips as he bounced his crotch against her bottom. The visceral horror replayed in her mind, accompanied by the sickening echo of her father's animalistic grunts.

'But I… I don't. I couldn't have.' Her voice came out on a horrified whisper. 'I have a rule.'

The sights, the sounds, even the smell—of furtive arousal, sordid sex—assaulted her senses as if she had walked into her father's office ten minutes ago, instead of ten years. She clapped her hands over her mouth as the gorge churning in her stomach surged up her throat.

'I'm going to puke.'

'So you didn't sleep with her, eh?' Phil snarled. 'You lying son of…'

Rye tuned out his friend's observations about his parentage as he watched Maddy dash to the toilets as if the hounds of hell were snapping at her heels.

Okay. Maybe he'd underestimated the size of this particular hurdle.

CHAPTER TEN

MADDY held her aching stomach and blinked at her reflection in the bathroom mirror.

Hello, Bride of Frankenstein.

Luckily, she hadn't had time to eat breakfast yet, so the dry heaves hadn't produced much. But the sallow skin of her face and the dark circles under her eyes made her look an absolute fright. Her ribs protested as she bent down to splash water onto her cheeks.

She straightened at the sound of someone entering behind her.

'I borrowed these from Phil.' Rye stood inside the door, holding a toothbrush wrapped in cellophane and a new tube of toothpaste. 'He keeps them for sleepover emergencies,' he added wryly.

She snatched the offerings out of his hand, determined not to be touched by the thoughtful gesture. 'You can't come in here. This is the Ladies.'

His eyebrow lifted. 'Yes, I can. I own the place, remember.'

'Thanks for the reminder.' She braced herself for the instinctive gagging reflex. Strangely, it didn't come.

She ripped open the toothbrush and applied the toothpaste, ignoring his silent, watchful presence. But, as she brushed her teeth, she felt painfully self-conscious. Even after all they'd done together, the mundane ritual seemed too personal to perform in front of him.

She rinsed her mouth and retied her ponytail. Great, she still looked like the Bride of Frankenstein, just with fresher breath.

'That was a very extreme reaction to the news that I own the café.' He stood propped against the wall by the door, giving her a probing look. 'What caused it?'

Maddy's spine stiffened. No way. She wasn't answering that. If brushing her teeth in front of him was too intimate, talking about her childhood was a definite no-go area.

'I should go back to work,' she said dismissively. But as she went to step past him he took her arm.

'You've got the rest of the day off. Phil's already lined up a replacement. And you're not going anywhere until I know what happened.' His brows lowered. 'You looked as if you were about to pass out.'

She pulled her arm free, not sure she could cope with being interrogated right now. 'I was in shock.' That much was true. 'You should have told me you owned this place as soon as you knew I worked here.'

The frown deepened. 'Why would I? It wasn't relevant.'

'It was to me,' she said.

'Why?'

There was that probing look again. 'I don't have to answer that.'

He cupped her cheek as she tried to turn away. 'Did some guy hurt you? Someone who was employing you?'

His jaw clenched as he asked the question and she realised this was more than curiosity.

'No.' She shook off his hand. 'It's nothing like that. It's…' She hesitated. Ducked her head. She couldn't talk about this. Not to him. She barely knew him. But where was the familiar nausea to bolster her resolve? 'It's nothing. It was a long time ago and it doesn't matter any more.'

'Maddy, it matters.'

'Why?'

'Because, if we don't sort it out…whatever it is…I'll have to fire you.'

She gave a strangled gasp. 'You'll *what*?' Had he lost his marbles? But he didn't look insane. He looked determined. 'Why would you do that? I work really hard; I…'

'This has nothing to do with your work ethic and you know it.'

He touched her cheek. She slapped his hand away.

'Well, what *does* it have to do with?' Temper rose to strengthen her resolve instead. She couldn't afford to lose this job. And she didn't deserve to, just because she'd slept with him and then made a spectacle of herself.

'Sacking you is the only option,' he began in that reasonable tone he only employed when saying something outrageous, 'if you won't sleep with me because I'm your boss. We'll have to find another way.'

Her jaw dropped. Literally. If she hadn't known it was physically impossible, she would have sworn it hit the floor.

As she stood, trying to get her mind to engage, to say something coherent, the elderly customer she had served earlier barged through the bathroom's double doors.

'Oh, hello; are you all right, dear?' The lady adjusted the glasses on her nose and peered at Maddy. 'You look a little peaky, love.'

'I'm…'

Rye cleared his throat and the old dear noticed him too.

'Well, really, I don't think this is the place for you, young man.' She straightened like a schoolmarm telling off a particularly unruly pupil, the top of her head barely reaching Rye's chest. 'This is the Ladies, you know.'

'Is it, really?' Rye didn't even have the decency to blush.

'If you want to talk to your young lady,' she added, 'you should do it elsewhere.'

'I'm not his young…' Maddy yelped as Rye's fingers wrapped firmly round her upper arm.

'You're absolutely right,' he said as he shoved the door open with one arm and hauled Maddy through with the other. 'I'll take my young lady somewhere more private.'

'Let go of me,' she spat, struggling against his grip as he

set off down the corridor, those long fingers tightening on her arm like a vice.

His uneven stride did nothing to slow the pace as he marched her, none too gently, into Phil's office and slammed the door.

'Now, let's have it,' he said, his voice low as her back butted the carved pine. He propped one hand above her head, caging her in. 'I want to know what made you react like that.'

Outrage blinded her. 'How dare you haul me about like that!' She slapped her palms against his chest, pushed hard. He didn't budge. 'And I'm never sleeping with...'

His lips came down. Hard, fast, insistent. And the protest got stuck in her throat. Right alongside the resistance.

She gasped. Strong fingers angled her head to deepen the kiss and molten heat shot up from her core. Her hands flexed in the soft cotton of his T-shirt as the sure strokes spread the wildfire.

Her breath gushed out as he lifted his head, moisture flooding between her thighs but doing nothing to put out the fire. One large palm settled on her hip, steadying her.

'Never say never, Maddy. Not to me. Not when you don't mean it.'

'But I do mean it,' she stammered, but the denial sounded false, even to her.

The rough, callused pad of his thumb touched her cheekbone. She could hear the thunder of her own heartbeat, feel her pulse pummelling her neck as he traced the line of her jaw, pressed the flutter in her throat. 'No you don't,' he murmured.

She looked away, feeling the outline of his arousal against her belly. Her sex ached and tightened, ready to receive him. She realised vaguely she wasn't revolted by him. Her boss. But hideously turned on.

Shame mingled with longing, the unstoppable rush of response a betrayal. Of that little girl who had sworn to despise all the women in her father's life—so she wouldn't have to despise him.

'What happened? Tell me,' he coaxed.

'I have ethics, that's all,' she whispered. 'I don't think it's right.' She couldn't tell him. It would leave her vulnerable. Like that frightened child with the evidence of something she'd tried so hard to deny branded on her memory for ever.

'That wasn't ethics.' He lifted her face. 'I'd say it was more like a phobia. You were physically sick.'

Tears clogged her throat at the concern in his voice.

'I wasn't sick. It wasn't that bad. I'm just tired and I hadn't had breakfast and...' Her pathetic attempt to explain away what he had seen trailed into silence as he continued to study her, knowledge and understanding in his steely gaze. 'Can't you just forget it?' she asked.

'No, I can't.' He huffed out a laugh. 'I don't want to fire you, but I will, if that's the only way I can make love to you again without you throwing up all over me.'

She heard the wry amusement in his tone—and the note of arrogance.

'Who said we were going to make love again? When did I agree to that? Or don't I get a say?' The adamant statement sounded fairly ridiculous after the kiss they'd shared. But she didn't care.

He sent her a sceptical look. 'How about we manage one problem at a time here?'

'Excuse me, my choice of sexual partners is not a prob...'

'Why can't you talk about it?' he interrupted. 'Was it that bad?' The tender tone cut the lecture off in mid-flow.

She sighed. 'No, it wasn't bad. Just embarrassing.' Maybe reason would deflect him. 'Honestly, Rye. It's not that big a deal. It's silly.'

'Humour me.'

'Oh, for...' She bit back the curse. He looked more stubborn than ever.

She stared over Rye's shoulder at the wide surf-battered beach through Phil's office window—and felt cornered. It seemed the more she held out, the more tenacious he became. Maybe if she got it over with he'd lose interest and let her be.

'All right. But, I warn you, it's an incredibly boring story.' She took a shuddering breath.

Tell him quickly, with as little emotion as possible.

'When I was thirteen, I went to see my dad at his office. It was his birthday and I'd brought him a present. My mother had kicked him out of the house. Again. Two days before. So he was staying at a hotel. Anyway...' She fumbled to a halt.

Stop reciting your life story. He's not that interested.

'I wanted to surprise him and I walked in on him boffing his secretary.' She let out a breath. 'See, no big deal. It's ridiculous that I've always let it bother me so much. You're right. Talking about it made it much better, so thanks.'

She twisted, reached for the door handle. But his hand covered hers before she could escape. She went still, stared blindly as his palm wrapped around the back of her hand and squeezed. Her heart stuttered. And tears clogged her throat. Tears she couldn't shed.

Please don't say anything.

'That must have been one hell of a shock,' he said.

She blinked, the idiotic tears prickling. 'Not really.' Or it shouldn't have been. 'I already knew he couldn't be faithful. They argued about "his sluts", as my mother liked to call them, all the time.'

'Did you tell your mother?' he asked gently.

Maddy gave her head a swift shake and a lone tear slipped over her lid. 'God, no.' She brushed it away, hoping he hadn't seen it.

'What about your father? How did he react?'

'He shouted at me to wait outside.' She gave a hollow laugh. 'The poor secretary went crimson. I think she was a lot more horrified by my presence than he was.' Maddy trembled, remembering the hideousness of listening to the muffled sounds through the closed door, her hands shaking as she threw the carefully wrapped present in the bin. 'When he came out ten minutes later he was charming. Condescending.' Was that the first time she had noticed how condescending? 'He told me he had needs that my mother had never been able to satisfy. But that didn't mean he didn't love her.'

It still disgusted her, she realised, the memory of his

chiselled features, flushed and satisfied. The musty scent of sex and sweat that clung to his linen suit as he hugged her and told her lies. 'He took me out for lunch to our favourite restaurant.'

And chose not to notice she couldn't eat a thing.

'Then he took me home. He persuaded my mother to take him back a week later, with a little extra help from a luxury trip to Paris. And it was never mentioned again.'

Rye's hand stroked down her hair, settled on her nape. 'Maddy, look at me.'

She turned to see sympathy and annoyance in his eyes. 'So you never spoke to anyone about it?'

'I spoke to Cal. Years later.'

His brow creased. 'Who's Cal?'

A weak smile tilted her lips. If she didn't know better, she'd think he was jealous. 'My brother. He's a barrister.'

The crease disappeared. 'So what did Cal say?'

'To get over it and move on.' If only she could have.

'But you couldn't,' he said with a perceptiveness that stunned her. 'So you made up your rule. About never sleeping with your boss.'

'It seemed like the best way to handle it.' Although the whole idea sounded hopelessly immature now. She blew out a breath, her body relaxing against the door. 'I can't believe I told you all that,' she murmured. Or how easy it had been. 'You must think I'm nuts, to let something that happened so long ago upset me.'

He brushed her hair back, framing her face. 'Are you still feeling sick?'

She curled her lip under her teeth and slowly shook her head, amazed. The memory that had tormented her for so long seemed pathetic now, rather than nauseating.

'Are you sure about that?' He lowered his head, brushed a kiss over her lips. The dart of fire arrowed down. 'Because I don't want you to start gagging again.'

She huffed out a laugh at the audacious statement, dizzy with relief. 'I hope you're not suggesting we have sex?' The words came out in a breathless rush as his hand swept under her T-shirt.

'Not at all.' He angled her head, nibbled kisses along her jaw. 'This isn't sex. It's immersion therapy.'

'Immersion..?' She gasped as he released her bra and cradled the swollen flesh of her breast in one hot palm.

'I want to be inside you, Maddy,' he said, toying with the sensitive peak.

Her thigh muscles tensed, the delicious buzz fading at the bold statement—and the memory of the first time he'd been inside her.

'I don't think that will work,' she mumbled, pulling away from him and smoothing down the T-shirt.

'Why not?' he asked, resting his hands on her hips.

'It's just…' She paused, heat pumping into her cheeks. *Talk about awkward.*

'You're a bit too…' She glanced down at the telltale ridge in his trousers, which looked even more daunting than before. She chewed on her lip. 'We could do something else,' she ventured hopefully. But she didn't have a clue what to offer.

Given that he was about to burst out of his pants, Rye didn't know whether to laugh at Maddy's artless offer or howl with frustration. 'Damn. Was I that much of a clod?'

'It's not that,' she said, rushing the words as the pink flags in her cheeks got pinker. 'It's not your fault.'

A strange pang squeezed his chest as he realised she was trying to spare his feelings. The irony struck him first. Women had thrown themselves at him ever since he was sixteen. And he'd never had a single complaint. Apart from that one time with Marta.

Until now.

'It's a matter of biology,' she continued. 'And…um…anatomy,' she stuttered, so red now she was practically glowing. 'We just don't…' She trailed off, flicking another wary glance at his crotch. 'Fit. Very well.'

He gave a humourless laugh. A little stunned by the evidence of how inexperienced she was. He'd liked her innocence yesterday, because it had made him feel superior and helped to repair his battered ego. He didn't feel so good about it now.

Had he seriously accused her of sleeping with Phil? He'd be astonished if she'd slept with more than a couple of guys in her whole life. That they hadn't delivered in the sack went without saying—or why would she be so clueless about sex?

He wondered if the childhood trauma she'd described had anything to do with her inexperience, then dismissed the thought. No need to go there.

He'd got her to talk about the incident to remove any barriers to them sleeping together again. The swell of anger and empathy when she'd recounted her father's sickening behaviour wasn't significant. He didn't want to think about that traumatised little girl or feel bad for her.

'Maddy.' He settled his hand on her nape, felt the punch of her pulse beneath his thumb and tried to come up with a way to explain the situation without sounding condescending. 'I'm not a small guy; I know that. But, believe me, we'll fit together fine.'

'How do you…?'

He pressed his finger to her lips, silencing her. 'I was rough. I didn't give you time to adjust. That's why it was so uncomfortable.' He dropped his hand, her widening eyes crucifying him.

'But I don't…' she began.

'I'll be careful this time.'

'But what if…'

'Maddy—' he cut her off, skimming soft flesh as his hand cruised under her T-shirt '—I can do better, I swear.' He pulled her flush against him, cradling the painful bulge in his jeans against her stomach and touched his lips to her forehead. 'Will you trust me?'

He almost added that he knew what he was doing, but stopped himself. Seeing her hesitate, seeing the wary confusion in her eyes, he wasn't so sure he did know what he was doing. When had he ever wanted a woman with this much intensity?

He forced the thought away.

She was sweet, sexy and vulnerable in a way he'd never encountered before. But the urgency, the driving need to have her again was only because, for the first time in a long time, he had something to prove.

Maddy flattened her palms against Rye's chest, felt the rapid ticks of his heartbeat matching her own and couldn't bring herself to say no.

No man had ever looked at her with such need before. As if they'd die from wanting her. She could see the tension in his jaw, the way his pupils had dilated to turn the vivid blue black with desire, and feel the outline of the disturbingly large erection.

'All right, if you're sure it'll be okay?'

He chuckled, the deep throaty sound sending a ripple of awareness down her spine. 'It'll be more than okay.'

His hands moved lower—but, when he flipped open the button on her jeans, she grabbed his wrist. 'Wait. We can't do it here. In Phil's office? In broad daylight?'

He smiled. 'Sure we can.'

'But…' Before the objection could take shape, he silenced the protest, covering her lips with his. Her head bumped against the door, the slight click of the lock echoing like a mission bell.

His tongue probed, seeking, learning the contours of her mouth. Then he caught her bottom lip between his teeth. The tiny nip stung as he smiled at her.

'No one can see in unless they have binoculars. And Phil's not going to disturb us if he wants to keep his job.'

He bent to drag off her jeans and knickers, not waiting for a reply.

She stepped out of the garments in a daze of longing, the giddy rush of forbidden pleasure exciting her even more. When had she ever done anything so impulsive?

But, as he led her to the sofa, his hand clasped around hers, she felt her unfettered breasts sway under the unhooked bra, felt the hem of her T-shirt brush her naked thighs and the rush of air against her exposed sex—and stopped.

He looked over his shoulder, his eyebrow lifting a fraction.

'Why am I practically naked and you're fully clothed?' she said.

His grin widened as he nodded. 'Let's remedy the situation.' Crossing his arms, he grasped the hem of his T-shirt and lifted it over his head.

She stared at the play of muscles across his lean belly, then feasted on the sight of his beautifully sculpted chest. Wisps of hair grew around flat nipples, then tapered to a point that disappeared beneath his jeans.

Her tongue flicked out to moisten parched lips as he kicked off his loafers, untied his belt with practised efficiency and then propped himself on the arm of the sofa to strip off his jeans and boxer shorts. The mammoth erection sprung out from the nest of dark hair at his groin and she gaped.

She'd hoped he wouldn't be as big. No such luck.

She heard the rough chuckle and looked up into hungry, heavy-lidded eyes glittering with amusement. 'Stop worrying,' he murmured as he took her hand, tugged her towards him.

'Easy for you to say,' she replied as the ridge of flesh touched her belly like a hot iron, sending shockwaves eddying to her core.

He laughed, the sound rich and full. 'Let's get you naked so we can get to the good bit.'

Her T-shirt and bra followed his clothes to the floor, leaving her quivering with a heady combination of anticipation and dread.

'There now, isn't that better?' he said, the teasing glint still very much in evidence as one callused palm cupped her breast.

She sighed as he played with the rigid peak, ignoring the evidence of his arousal, still hot against her hip.

Then he dipped his head and circled the raw nerves with his tongue. She moaned, her fingers sinking into the soft waves of his hair as she luxuriated in the rough strokes of his tongue. Fire spiralled down, releasing slick juices as she trembled. Maybe a little discomfort was a small price to pay for this.

He lifted his head and she sucked in an unsteady breath as cooler air brushed her wet, fevered skin. Gripping her shoulders with firm hands, he turned her round until she felt the hot flesh butt against her bottom. He edged her forward, bending her over the sofa.

She quaked as the brutal erection touched the swollen folds of her sex. Feeling too exposed, too vulnerable, she tried to rise.

'Shh, it's okay,' he whispered, his hands stroking her back, cradling her buttocks as he gentled her. 'I can control the penetration better in this position.' Then he drew his fingers through the curls at her centre, finding the hard nub. A strangled cry escaped as her body arched against the exquisite torture.

His fingers continued to play, building the waves of ecstasy as she listened to the muffled sounds of him sheathing himself. She started, pulled out of the reverie as the head of his penis probed.

She groaned, the guttural sound a plea as he sank into her in one long, slow, relentless thrust. She panted, ecstasy receding to be replaced by a fullness, a stretched feeling more than she could bear. She opened her mouth to tell him to stop, to tell him it was too much.

But the protest died in her throat as his knowing fingers caressed her again. He touched, stroked, teased, holding still inside her, until the shocking pleasure made her buck, lodging him to the hilt.

She sobbed as he began to move. The short careful thrusts, getting longer, harder, more demanding as the sure, relentless swell of pleasure built. She cried out as the waves of ecstasy rushed up and rolled over her, then receded, only to build again without pause, without reason. He grasped her hips, establishing a relentless rhythm.

She soared upwards, the wave swelling and crashing like a tsunami now, tumbling her over and thundering down to hurl her into oblivion in one mindless rush of pure rapture.

CHAPTER ELEVEN

'I THINK I like immersion therapy.' Maddy grinned as the hair of Rye's chest tickled her cheek, his answering chuckle rumbling against her ear. They lay together on Phil's sofa, gloriously naked, Rye's long legs tangling with hers. She'd never felt more wanton or more wonderful in her life.

Who knew sex could be that spectacular?

His arm tightened across her shoulders as he peered down into her face. 'So I take it there were no ill effects this time?'

'Not one,' she replied enthusiastically. She stretched, the slight discomfort between her thighs nothing compared to the triumphant afterglow. The flush of contentment washed over her as she recalled how he'd eased into her so carefully and brought her to a stunning…

She bolted upright. 'Oh, my God.'

She stared in amazement at their surroundings. Phil's desk, piled high with papers, the shelves full of bulging file folders, the dying pot plant, even the deluxe sofa that they were now lounging on together, completely nude.

'Is something wrong?' Rye asked calmly.

'We just did it in Phil's office!'

He sent her an amused frown. 'I realise that.'

'And you're my boss…' She hesitated, briefly distracted by the glorious memory of him buried deep inside her.

He slung one arm behind his head, skimmed his palm down her back to rest on her buttock. 'Very observant,' he said, amusement lightening his voice.

'Rye, don't you see the significance? I'm cured.'

'Cured of what?'

She placed her hand on her stomach. 'I don't feel nauseous, or even weird about it. I feel wonderful.'

'Good,' he said, caressing her bottom. 'But what is it you don't feel weird about?'

'What I saw my father doing to his secretary. It doesn't matter any more. I don't care.' She settled back down, loving the feel of his chest hair abraiding sensitive nipples, and kissed him on the jaw. 'Rye, you cured me.' She beamed at him, delighting in the feeling of recklessness, of freedom.

He laughed, stroking her rump. 'Glad to be of service.'

Maddy laughed at his smug tone. Then shivered.

Rye took her shoulders and lifted her off him. 'Come on.' He sat up and scooped her T-shirt off the floor. 'As much as I enjoy ogling your naked body,' he said, his eyes slipping suggestively to her breasts as he handed her the T-shirt, 'it's getting chilly in here.'

She whipped the garment over her head, pushing the sudden feeling of disappointment to one side.

This was finally it, then. Her wanton fling was well and truly over. They'd done the wild thing until they'd got it right. But, now they had, there wasn't anything else to explore.

They got dressed in companionable silence but, as Maddy glimpsed Rye's tight, muscular butt disappearing behind cotton boxers, she couldn't help letting out a sigh.

Why did Mr Wrong have to be such a stud muffin?

It was very obvious from Rye's expertise with women, his unassailable self-confidence in bed and the dominating arrogance that had allowed him to march into the café and demand she sleep with him again, that she was just one in a very long line of conquests. He'd been thoughtful when she'd almost thrown up in front of him, and surprisingly sensitive while coaxing the truth about her aversion to sleeping with her boss out of her. But she wasn't about to kid herself. In a day or two he would have moved on to someone else.

She pushed away the little pang of regret. And the knowledge that it would take her a great deal longer to forget him.

She firmed her lips and retied her ponytail, making herself look away as he tugged his T-shirt over his head and covered up that magnificent chest.

Don't get sentimental, silly. This is your endorphins talking.

Of course she wouldn't forget him as easily. Because no man had ever excited her, or made her feel the way he did in bed. But all the qualities that made him so great in bed also made him all wrong for her in every other way.

Sitting on the sofa, she put on her trainers.

She had never been the sentimental type. And she knew, from witnessing the agony of her parents' marriage for years, that passion didn't last. You needed compatibility and companionship and something tangible in common to base a real relationship on. Great sex, even spectacular sex, wasn't enough. However drop dead gorgeous Ryan King might be, and however accomplished in the sack, she knew virtually nothing about him, and what she did know suggested he wasn't the guy for her.

'What are you thinking?'

She glanced round to see Rye sitting beside her, his injured leg stretched out in front of him.

'Nothing,' she replied, not about to relay her thoughts.

A casual fling was a casual fling and it was a little lowering to realise that she hadn't quite been able to accept it at face value, even though she knew she should.

He laid a hand on her knee, rubbed gently. 'Are you sure?'

She sent him a rueful smile—for a sex machine, the man could be quite sensitive. 'Positive.' She covered his hand with hers.

He looked down at their joined hands and she felt him stiffen almost imperceptibly.

She lifted her hand, knowing she'd crossed some invisible barrier without meaning to.

He looked away but, just as she felt a prickle of unease, he spoke. 'You shouldn't let what your parents did matter,' he said, his voice distant but sincere.

His eyes met hers and for one brief moment she thought she saw a pain so raw and so all-consuming it took her breath away.

'They can screw you up,' he said, the tone dull and flat, the flash of pain gone as if it had never been. 'But only if you let them.'

'I see,' she replied. But she didn't see, not really. And suddenly she wanted to. Maybe this was only a casual fling, but he'd probed into her past this morning; why shouldn't she probe his? 'What were *your* parents like?'

'Mine?' His eyes widened. 'Who knows?' He gave a careless shrug. 'I hardly remember them. They died when I was twelve.'

'Oh, Rye, I'm so sorry.' Sympathy assailed her. 'That must have been terrible.' Her own parents had been selfish and self-absorbed but, whatever their shortcomings, it would have been harder to be without them. 'Did you have brothers or sisters?'

'No. My grandfather took me in. That's how I ended up in Cornwall at Trewan Manor.'

'Where did you live before that?' she asked, unable to control her curiosity at her first insight into his life.

'All over. Hawaii. California. Cozumel for a while.'

So that explained the odd American word or phrase, the lazy cadence of his speech.

'My parents didn't do conventional,' he said conversationally, slipping on his loafers. 'We lived out of a camper van and followed the surf. Dad called us the three spirits.' His eyes had gone dark with memory. 'It was a stupid joke, but it made her laugh every time he said it.'

Maddy's heart pounded. He sounded so matter-of-fact. So detached. But why had he lied, saying he barely remembered his parents when it was obvious the loss still hurt?

She touched her hand to his back. 'You still miss them?'

'What?' The shadow cleared from his eyes as he twisted round, dislodging her hand. 'Hardly. They died nearly twenty years ago.' He pushed himself up, steadied himself on his injured leg. 'Believe me, I'm not that sentimental.'

He said the word as if it were offensive.

'Let's go.' Offering her his hand, he hauled her up. 'Before Phil starts banging on the door.'

As he escorted her out of Phil's office, his face carefully blank, it occurred to Maddy that she had a hundred and one questions she wanted to ask him. How had his parents died? Had his grandfather filled the gap? And what had it felt like to be cast adrift in Cornwall, in that austere, forbidding house on the cliff after a warm, loving childhood spent with parents who even she could tell from those two brief sentences had adored him and adored each other?

Was it harder to have what she'd always dreamed of—a warm, loving home and parents who cared about you—and then have it torn away, than never to have it at all?

'Maddy, you're not doing that thinking thing again, are you?' he said lightly, his hand settling on the small of her back as they walked down the corridor towards the café.

She sent him a weak smile. 'I'm just wondering how I'm going to look Phil in the eye,' she said, knowing she couldn't ask any of the questions buzzing in her head. She had no right to ask them. And she doubted he would answer them anyway.

'We'll have to come up with a convincing story about what we've been doing all this time,' she added. 'Or he's never going to let me forget it.'

'Phil will have figured it out. And, anyway, it's not a secret.'

The note of arrogance, of entitlement, reminded her he was still the boss.

'I'd rather he didn't know, though. Don't worry, I'll think of something.'

'No, you won't. If he hasn't guessed already, I'll tell him.'

She stopped to stare at him. 'But you can't.'

'Why can't I?'

'Because I work here.' Was he really that dense?

'So?' He shrugged. 'You're entitled to a sex life.'

'Even so…' She scrambled for another reason. She needed to keep their fling private. However casual it had been for Rye, it hadn't been quite as casual for her. She intended to work on that. But she couldn't bear it if they became the subject of kitchen gossip. 'I don't want Phil to know.'

She took a careful breath, but came up short when he took hold of her arm.

'Maddy,' he said curtly, 'don't tell me you're under the impression this is over?'

'But…' She saw the muscle twitch in his jaw, which she already knew signalled his arousal. And, just like that, her thigh muscles melted and the still tender spot between her legs began to throb. 'But why would you want to do it with *me* again?'

As soon as the words were out of her mouth, she wanted to claw them back and bury them in a very deep hole.

He'd taken her to nirvana, more than once. But she wasn't about to delude herself that she'd done the same for him. She wasn't that good at sex and she knew it. Still, she wished she hadn't told him as much. It made her sound needy and pathetic.

She winced. 'Could you pretend you didn't hear that?' she said, hideously humiliated.

He shook his head slowly, studying her with what, she had an awful feeling, might be pity.

She waited. So mortified she wanted to die on the spot. But, instead of laughing at her, or saying something condescending, his eyes narrowed and, for an insane moment, she thought she saw a flash of fury.

Rye curled his fingers into a fist. What he'd like to do right now was hunt down the bastards who had destroyed Maddy's confidence and throttle them on the spot. He shoved his hand into the back pocket of his jeans.

She was actually serious. He could see it in her face, and the flush of embarrassment lighting up her cheeks. She had no idea she'd blown him away. He wanted to tell her that she was the most refreshing, the most artlessly sexy and seductive woman he'd ever encountered, but how could he do that and not make this sound like more than it was?

Something he couldn't afford to do.

Because he'd already made a mess of this. He was usually so clear with women about what he wanted out of a relationship. And what he didn't. He set boundaries and he never crossed them. No point in confusing things and setting yourself up for an ugly scene further down the line. But he'd crossed those boundaries with Maddy. In fact, he'd never even set them. Because he'd been distracted by his own needs.

After their little heart-to-heart in Phil's office, when he'd blurted out that rubbish about his parents, he'd known he needed to start setting those boundaries now. And make it clear he wasn't comfortable with that level of intimacy.

But she was looking at him now, her eyes shadowed with embarassment. As if she couldn't believe he really wanted to sleep with her again. And he didn't have a clue how to say what he had to without knocking her confidence even more.

'Maddy.' He cupped her cheek, felt the instinctive tremor of response and knew he wasn't finished with her. Not by a long shot. But he had a tightrope to walk now. And he was doing it blindfolded. 'I thought you enjoyed yourself this time?'

Those luminous green eyes widened even more. 'I did. You know I did.'

'Then what's the problem with us enjoying more of the same?'

He settled his hand on her shoulder, skimmed his thumb across her collarbone and felt the flutter of her pulse.

'But…'

'I'm not looking for anything serious,' he said casually, but watched her reaction like a hawk.

She seemed more confused than upset by the suggestion. 'I know that,' she said, surprising him a little.

'I'm going to be in Cornwall for another month or so,'

he added, careful not to imply that he would be around indefinitely.

The truth was he had no concrete plans to return to London. He'd left the company in capable hands and had been content to forget about it while living like a recluse in his grandfather's house. One of the things he'd resolutely refused to think about was his future, because he'd been so busy dwelling on his past. Apart from the fact that his behaviour now seemed remarkably boring and self-indulgent, it occurred to him that if he was going to indulge himself with Maddy, he needed to put an end date into the equation.

'I still have some recuperation to do but, once winter sets in, I'll be returning to London.' For the first time in a long time, the thought didn't make his stomach tighten with dread. 'But until then, I don't see why we can't continue to enjoy ourselves.'

'I don't…' She stopped, clearly lost for words.

'We could give each other a great deal of pleasure in that time. Why deny ourselves when there's no need?'

A small line of concentration formed on her brow. He felt the pulse of heat in his crotch. Damn, she really was adorable. And completely unique. When was the last time he'd had to put this much effort into getting a woman into his bed?

'What do you say to a no-strings affair? We spend a few weeks exploiting the great sexual chemistry between us and then go our separate ways. And nobody gets hurt.'

Those round green eyes met his. 'No strings. No promises. Just great sex?'

'That's correct.'

Rye felt the punch of his own heartbeat as he waited for her reply. The smile died as he began to feel a little uneasy. Had he ever been this desperate for a woman to say yes?

'All right,' she said, as if mulling the idea over in her mind. 'I think that would be fun.'

'Great.'

He gripped her waist, hauled her up for a kiss, relief and euphoria lifting the moment of discomfort.

She giggled, then the little line returned to her brow as he set her back on her feet. 'Can I ask you for one promise, though, Rye?'

His heart sank at the thoughtful tone of voice. Promises were top of his list of things to avoid in a relationship. 'Sure,' he said cautiously, hoping like hell whatever she had in mind wasn't going to be a deal-breaker.

'Promise me,' she said gently, 'we'll never pretend this is something it's not.'

The breath he hadn't realised he'd been holding gushed out. 'You have my word,' he replied, pleased her promise would be so easy to keep.

'Good.' She sent him a tentative smile, the look on her face a tantalising combination of bashful and eager. 'I could cook you dinner at the cottage tonight,' she said, the sparkle in her green eyes making his breath catch. 'And we can discuss terms.'

He chuckled. 'I'm there.' Tightening his arms round her waist, he kissed her again. 'What time do you want me?' he said, his heart soaring at the prospect of a decent meal in fascinating company after so many months eating convenience food alone.

'Get there at seven.' She tapped a fingernail to his chest, her eyes smoky with desire. 'I'll let you know when I want you later.'

He laughed at the saucy comment as the blood rushed straight to his groin.

Damn, but it was good to be back in the world of the living at last.

CHAPTER TWELVE

MADDY glared at the gloopy mess in her saucepan and felt the snakes in her stomach tangle themselves into giant knots.

Her béchamel had curdled. How could her béchamel have curdled when she'd made it about a billion times before? She pressed her hand to her stomach and took two careful breaths.

Perhaps because her nerves were stretched so tight they were about to snap.

Why on earth had she invited Rye to dinner? It had seemed like such a great idea at the time.

Her hormones had still been fizzy like a bottle of shaken cola and her confidence soaring into the stratosphere at the knowledge that he still wanted her. When he'd made the offer of a no-strings affair and she'd blithely agreed, the endorphin rush had blinded her to all the possible pitfalls.

No strings, no promises meant no expectations. Which was just what she wanted. Why he should want her so much, she had no idea, but she wasn't about to look that gift horse in the mouth a second time. When was she ever likely to get an offer like this again? And the chance to dynamite herself out of the rut she'd been in for years?

She could avail herself of Rye King's superstar abilities in bed and spice up her sadly mundane sex life for the next few weeks and all she had to do was enjoy the ride.

It was way past time she put Maddy first for a change. It all made perfect sense. Or so she'd thought at the time.

She'd offered him a home-cooked meal because she loved cooking. It relaxed her. And inviting him to the cottage gave her the home advantage. She'd planned to be nicely mellow and totally in charge of the situation before they jumped each other tonight.

But what she hadn't counted on was the crows of doubt swooping down and pecking apart her logic once the dizzying rush of lust from their nooner in Phil's office had cleared.

What if she'd made a catastrophic mistake? Was she really capable of handling a man as overpowering as Ryan King? She had absolutely no experience of the kind of fling he was talking about, while he was clearly an expert at them. And how was overdosing on endorphins on a regular basis going to affect her common sense?

The first crow to appear had been Phil. She'd insisted on finishing her shift, hoping against hope that Phil would be too chivalrous to mention her and Rye's twenty-minute disappearing act. No such luck. Although Rye hadn't helped her chances one bit with the deliberately proprietary kiss he'd planted on her lips in front of the whole café—garnering a round of applause from the customers and a scowl from his manager—before he strolled out of the door, the hitch in his stride taking on a definite swagger.

Maddy had nipped off to the kitchen, but Phil had cornered her by the wait station ten minutes later.

'Maddy, what the hell do you think you're playing at?' he'd demanded.

'I don't know what you mean,' she replied, struggling for guileless but failing miserably with the heat throbbing in her cheeks after Rye's kiss.

'Don't give me that. Knowing Rye, I can guess what you two were up to in my office.'

The denial clogged in her throat as the heat in her cheeks went nuclear.

'Yeah, I thought so,' Phil finished, shaking his head.

'I'm sorry,' she blurted out. Why did the liberating experience of ten minutes ago seem hopelessly immature and impetuous all of a sudden?

'Don't be,' he said, resigned. 'It's not your fault. Rye has that effect on women. He always has. Even when we were in school. He could have any girl he wanted. The rest of us were in awe.'

Maddy swallowed. While she appreciated this insight into Rye's teenage years, Phil wasn't telling her anything she hadn't already guessed. And, frankly, knowing about Rye's success with women from such an early age was making her nervous.

'But he never kept any of them,' Phil said, his voice sombre. 'And some of them tried really hard to hang on to him.' He sighed. 'Whatever he's told you, whatever promises he's made, he won't keep them. I love the guy like a brother. But, when it comes to women, he's about as dependable as Casanova on Viagra.'

The knots of tension in Maddy's shoulders tightened. She really didn't need to hear this.

'It's okay, Phil. I know what I'm doing.' Or at least she hoped she did. 'You don't have to worry.'

Phil shrugged, looking resigned. 'Fine; I guess I can't stop you.' He leant down and gave her a brotherly kiss on the forehead. 'But make sure you don't fall for him. Because the only one whose heart will get broken is yours.'

Maddy huffed out a laugh at the memory of Phil's parting comment as she plucked the whisk off the utensils rack. Who would have guessed that Phil had such a romantic streak? She started attacking the lumps in her béchamel as the snakes in her stomach began to calm down.

Phil's little speech may have made her a little too aware of the magnitude of what she had agreed to. And how much more experienced Rye was in bed. But, thank goodness, falling for her no-strings fling was one problem she didn't have to worry about.

She wasn't a romantic. And she never would be. She had seen what the 'love delusion', as Cal liked to call it, had done to her parents. Hadn't they always professed to love each other while tearing each other apart?

She stared out of the window at the dusky evening light. She had no delusions about love. Because the experience of living through the carnage of her parents' marriage had made her positive it didn't exist.

Yes, one day she yearned to have a stable, steady relationship and make a home she could be proud of—with a man who respected her and cared for her. A man she could trust implicitly. In a way her mother had never been able to trust her father.

But she already knew Rye wasn't that man and she wasn't enough of a fool any more to think she could mould him into that man with enough time and effort and patience on her part.

Tonight would set the tone for the weeks to come. And the only reason she was so nervous was that she wanted to get it right. She wanted to be confident and in control, but also sexy and alluring and irresistible. She took a deep breath and let it out slowly. Which meant she had to relax.

She poured the still gloopy but just about passable sauce onto her lasagne.

Basically, she wanted to be Mata Hari. She layered the vegetables she'd roasted with the sheets of pasta. With a little pinch of domestic goddess for added flavour. She slipped the completed lasagne into the oven. Which was a tall order for any woman, especially a woman who'd spent most of her love life so far being Minnie Mouse.

Then she spotted the time on the oven clock.

Six thirty-five!

Whipping out the tea towel tucked into her jeans and dumping it on the counter top, Maddy dashed into the cottage's shoe-box-sized bedroom.

She had less than half an hour to turn Minnie Mouse into Mata Hari, Domestic Goddess.

Maddy jumped at the buzz of the doorbell and swept damp palms down the simple black dress she'd settled on after trying on three different outfits. Pulling one of the silk designs she'd painted this spring off the top shelf, she used it as a scarf to tie her hair back hastily, drew a few curls down to frame her face and hoped it made her look sexy. Slipping into her matching black pumps, she crossed the front room and pulled open the heavy oak door.

Rye's broad shoulders blocked out the evening light as his gaze dropped down her figure. The dress didn't have much of a cleavage, but heat still crept up her chest at the thorough perusal.

'Hello, Madeleine,' he said, the husky tone of voice deliberately suggestive. He handed her the bottle of wine he had tucked under his arm. 'I bought French Merlot. I hope it suits whatever you're serving.'

She glanced at the label. The wine looked pricey and sophisticated—and far too good for the mess she had in the oven. 'This'll be great.' She beat a hasty retreat, clutching the wine in her fist. His uneven tread sounded on the wooden floor behind her and she forced herself to slow down.

Relax. Focus.

She sucked in a hasty breath.

And remember to breathe, Mata Hari, before you pass out.

She plonked the bottle on the small pine table she'd laid in the front room with her grandmother's best bone china and made herself face him. He looked impossibly large in the cosy confines of the sitting room, his head skimming the exposed beams on the ceiling. How come she'd never noticed how tall he was until now? He had to be at least six foot three.

'I made vegetarian lasagne.' She fiddled with one of the knives, straightened it, before clasping her hands together. 'I hope you haven't any objections to aubergine.'

His lips quirked. 'Not that I know of,' he said, amusement lightening his voice. He wore a black leather jacket, a dark blue T-shirt and black jeans, one hip raised in a casual stance as he surveyed the room.

So much for having the home advantage. She was wound

tighter than a coiled spring and he couldn't have looked more relaxed, dominating the small space as if he owned it.

His eyes came back to hers. 'Where did you get the seascape?' he asked, nodding past her shoulder as he shrugged off the jacket and slung it over the back of a chair. 'It's stunning.'

She glanced round, but knew the picture he was referring to. She'd painted it last autumn, not long after she and Steve had broken up. 'I did it,' she replied, relaxing a little; small talk was good. It would help her focus. 'It's a silk painting, actually.'

He stepped up to the artwork. She drew in a sharp breath as the soft hairs of his forearm brushed against her, enveloping her in the tantalising scent of musk and man and pheromones.

'You're an artist,' he murmured. 'And a remarkably talented one.'

She flushed, surprised by the compliment and how much it meant to her. The silk painting had only ever been a hobby. 'Thank you.'

'Why were you angry?' he asked, his eyes fixing on hers.

'How can you tell?' she said, stunned again by how perceptive he was. She dragged her gaze away to look at the painting. Her anger at Steve and at herself was clearly visible in the choppy crest and spikes of the waves, the glowering clouds on the horizon. The weather hadn't been particularly turbulent that day, as far as she could remember, but she had been.

She jumped slightly as a warm hand settled on her nape.

'You keep surprising me, Maddy. And I'm not easily surprised.'

Electricity raced down her spine and her nipples pebbled into hard points as his fingers stroked up her neck.

He turned her towards him and she braced her hands on his chest. 'Is that a bad thing?' she said breathlessly.

'A bad thing? Not at all.' His lips skimmed across hers, the touch barely there. She strained towards him instinctively, her bottom lip quivering.

'Why are you so nervous?' he murmured.

'I...' she stuttered. He was so close she could see the flecks of silver in his irises, taste the peppermint on his breath. So much for Mata Hari. One kiss and he was very definitely in charge. 'I'm feeling a bit overwhelmed,' she said truthfully.

'I see.' He chuckled and his mouth closed the tiny gap.

Her fingers sank into the silky strands of his hair as his lips travelled down to devour her neck. Her head dropped back to give him better access, her whole body vibrating with need, excitement finally drowning out her trepidation. And then her nose wrinkled and she drew in a deep breath… Of burnt lasagne.

'The dinner,' she yelped as she scrambled out of his arms.

She raced across the room with his laughter echoing in her ears.

So much for the domestic goddess too.

'It's ruined.' She dumped the charred remains of her signature dish onto the hob and batted away the acrid smoke.

'Maybe just a bit.' He laid his palm on the small of her back and passed her a glass of the Merlot.

She took a hasty swallow to ease the mortification tightening her throat—and nearly choked.

His palm rubbed circles on her back through the cotton of her dress. 'It's not a problem. I'll order take-out from the hotel restaurant, get one of the waiters to drive it up.'

She placed the glass on the sideboard, her shoulders slumping. Who was she kidding? She wasn't cut out for this. She didn't do sophisticated, or sensual.

'I'm so sorry, Rye. But I'm not sure this is going to work.'

His eyebrow lifted and he looked so damn gorgeous she wanted to bawl her eyes out. Why couldn't she be the sort of woman who could have her cake and eat it too? Or, at the very least, bake it without burning it to a crisp.

'All this over burnt lasagne.' He gave her an easy smile, not looking deterred in the least. 'It's not important, Maddy. As sweet as it was for you to offer, I don't expect you to cook for me.'

'I know. It's not that. It's…' She picked up her wine glass, watched the rich red liquid slop against the rim. 'I'm so nervous I'm shaking.'

He took the glass out of her hand, placed it carefully on the sideboard again.

'I mean, I've never done anything like this before,' she blurted out. 'I don't have a clue what I'm doing.'

He drew her neatly into his arms. She blinked, shocked to feel the outline of his erection. How could he be turned on when she'd made such a mess of things?

'You're over-complicating things,' he said, the low timbre of his voice making the hairs on her nape stand on end and every one of the places where their bodies touched throb. 'I know exactly what I'm doing,' he said, framing her face. 'So there's no need for you to worry about it.'

He threaded his fingers into her hair, held her head steady for a mind-numbing kiss. Her panic receded, blasted away by the rush of lust as his tongue worked its way into her mouth and then explored in soft, sensual strokes.

He broke away first, gave her a quick kiss on the nose. 'So why don't you relax and enjoy yourself and let me lead the way?'

'I'll try,' she said hesitantly, still feeling hopelessly overwhelmed.

He grinned suggestively and she gave a half-laugh. He looked so sinfully seductive.

'Don't worry, I happen to know a great relaxation technique.'

By the time the delivery of seared scallops and rocket salad arrived an hour later, Maddy was so relaxed she was practically in a coma—and ready to let Rye lead her anywhere he wanted to.

CHAPTER THIRTEEN

MADDY hummed the joyous chorus of an old R & B song as she pedalled past the gates of Trewan Manor. Leaves brushed across the pathway as the crisp autumnal air stung her cheeks. November had always been her favourite month of the year—brisk and exhilarating.

She swung her leg over the saddle and rode the pedal the final few metres to the house, picturing Rye's naked body in the cottage's tiny shower cubicle that morning. And having the hottest guy in the universe at her disposal certainly kept the cold at bay. A giggle popped out as she propped the bike against the front wall.

She stopped, blushing slightly.

Good grief, when had she become a giggler?

She grinned, hauling a sack of groceries out of the bike's front basket. Probably some time in the last two weeks. Having Rye King as a lover was likely to make any woman high. On life and endorphins. The man was a sexual athlete, of Olympic gold medal winning standards. Passionate, inventive, tireless and completely insatiable. She hugged the groceries to her chest, a delicious shiver running through her at the memory of exactly what he'd done to her in the shower that morning.

The grin got bigger as she practically floated to the Manor's front door, adding dedicated, attentive and extremely flexible to his list of accomplishments. She gave a breathy sigh. Rye made love with a concentration so intense it made her feel as if she were the centre of his universe.

Her hand stilled on the door knocker. And the wide grin faltered.

Okay, maybe that was a teensy, weensy bit over the top. Even for a woman who'd been overdosing on endorphins for a fortnight. She shrugged. Clearly blow-your-socks-off sex had the ability to make you lose your grip on reality occasionally. Good to know.

She wasn't the centre of Rye King's universe. Any more than he was the centre of hers. All they'd really shared in the last two weeks was a string of intimate meals and even more intimate sexual liaisons. For, while her senses had become attuned to every aspect of his body—his musky enticing scent, the sweet salty taste of his skin, the silky softness of the thin line of hair that bisected his six-pack and made him tense when she trailed her fingertip down it—she still knew next to nothing else about him.

Because the man guarded personal information with the same focus and concentration that he made love. And, frankly, she'd had enough of it. She shifted the groceries onto one arm and lifted the Manor's heavy brass knocker. But all that was about to change.

She was here now on a mission—having decided that his evasiveness whenever she asked a personal question was getting ridiculous.

When they'd first embarked on their casual affair, she'd totally respected his boundaries. Their no-strings fling was about having fun and... She paused. How had Rye put it? Oh, yeah, 'exploiting the great sexual chemistry' between them. And that had been absolutely fine. At first.

In the beginning, she'd had no desire to examine his psyche, to expose the secrets of his past, especially as he seemed so averse to the idea. So she'd backed off every time she saw that shuttered look that told her louder than words she'd just strayed into forbidden territory. Plus Rye was extremely adept at distracting her. And she'd found it next to impossible not to let him.

But the fact was, after spending every night together at the cottage for two whole weeks, they were starting to run out of things to talk about.

She pounded on the door and guilty knowledge lifted the hairs on the back of her neck.

Stop lying to yourself, Westmore.

All right, fine. Her decision to surprise him this evening had nothing to do with a small talk shortage. And everything to do with the fact that her curiosity was starting to strangle her.

She wasn't usually a nosy parker. But, the more circumspect Rye became, the more desperate she was to know why he found it necessary to be so secretive. Those questions that had buzzed around in her brain after their tryst in Phil's office a fortnight ago were all still there. With several more added.

Why was he so determined to keep her at arm's length? What was so terrifying about revealing personal information? Why wouldn't he talk about even the most innocuous details of his childhood? And why had he resolutely refused to invite her back to the Manor since that first night?

Yesterday evening, as he'd tucked into her chicken and asparagus risotto and she'd studied the way his wavy hair had begun to curl around his ears, all the questions queuing up on the tip of her tongue had been about to choke her.

His brooding intensity, the moody, taciturn quality that lurked beneath the relaxed, easy-going charm fascinated her. So much so that getting to know and understand him was starting to become an obsession.

But it was this morning's events that had finally spurred her into action.

While she'd brushed her teeth, Rye had appeared in the bathroom in his boxers, hugged her round the waist and told her he had an important conference call first thing in the morning so he'd have to stay at his place tonight.

She'd tried to dismiss the little bump of dismay at the thought of spending her first night without him as nothing more than endorphin withdrawal. But she couldn't dismiss the stab of disappointment—and hurt—that it hadn't even occurred to him to invite her over to the Manor.

She'd been about to suggest it herself when he'd started murmuring in that low, sexy voice about making up for lost time, pressed her against the shower cubicle to nibble the pulse in her neck—and, before she knew it, she'd been flooding the bathroom instead. She'd still been draped across the bed, seeing stars, her wet hair soaking the quilt when she'd heard the rumble of his car engine as he drove off.

It had taken her a full half an hour more, while she got dressed and put away the breakfast dishes, before she'd finally cottoned on to the fact that their mind-blowing water aerobics had been yet another of Rye's expertly deployed distraction techniques.

The realisation had annoyed her, frustrated her and been the final straw.

Right, pal. Two can play at that game.

The plan she'd come up with while repairing the extensive damage to the bathroom was both simple and satisfying and wonderfully empowering.

She heard the clank of the bolt on the Manor's door unlocking. A sweet and she hoped only slightly smug smile tilted her lips.

Before meeting Rye, she never would have had the guts to show up at a guy's house uninvited, no matter how much mind-altering sex they'd had together in the last fortnight. But being with Rye, having him want her with a power and a passion that hadn't dimmed in the slightest in the last two weeks had given her confidence a boost that she now planned to put to good use.

The door swung open.

Oh, my. There is a God.

Her pulse fluttered and her thigh muscles dissolved as she studied the magnificent sight before her. Perspiration glistened on his skin, highlighting the impressive contours of his bare chest and making the thin cotton athletic shorts cling to muscular thighs. The angry puckered scars above his left kneecap only enhanced his dangerous sex appeal.

'Maddy?' He lifted the towel slung round his neck to wipe his brow, his voice a little hoarse. 'Sorry, I was in the gym. I didn't hear the door.'

Maddy's smile widened as she inhaled the intoxicating smell of pheromones and sweat. 'I come bearing gifts,' she said, holding up her carefully selected bag of bribes. 'I thought I'd cook you dinner here for a change.' She dipped her eyelashes. 'Then we can discuss dessert.'

She sashayed past him, knowing the new black jeans outlined her bum to perfection. Was it her imagination or had he looked less sure of himself than usual?

He gave a strained chuckle as he closed the door behind her.

The feeling of power made her a little light-headed. She'd cornered him on his home turf as planned; now all she had to do was torture him until he lost the will to resist.

Good Lord, was that a thong peeking over the waistband of her jeans?

Rye cursed under his breath as Maddy strolled down the hallway ahead of him, swaying her slim hips like a courtesan.

He took several deep breaths and tried to focus on the dull ache in his thigh from the punishing physiotherapy instead of the growing ache in his crotch.

Take your eyes off her backside, King, before all the blood drains out of your brain.

He tried to muster some irritation at the surprise visit. He'd been punishing himself for over an hour on those damn weight machines to stop from fixating on all the things he had convinced himself he should not be doing with Maddy this evening—and now she'd shot all his hard work right to hell.

He stopped in the kitchen doorway and watched her shrug off her suede jacket to reveal a lacy little vest thing that moulded to her full breasts like a second skin. As she unloaded a bunch of plump red tomatoes from her shopping bag, her cleavage strained against the stretchy cotton.

He bit back a groan. This had to be the road to ruin because he could feel all his good intentions crashing and burning in a tidal wave of lust.

Unfortunately, he was finding it hard to care. One more night couldn't do that much harm after two solid weeks of unbridled indulgence. He'd simply start weaning himself off his addiction to Maddy Westmore tomorrow.

Best to be philosophical about it. Maybe having her here instead of in the cosy little cottage wasn't such a bad thing after all. He'd resisted the temptation to invite her to the Manor so far because the dark oppressive house always made him feel more vulnerable, more exposed.

And Maddy was proving to be quite the little busybody. Usually, when he made it clear he wasn't into share and discuss, women got bored or backed off. But not Maddy. She'd been relatively easy to put off at first but, as the days passed, she'd got more and more persistent. And he'd been finding it tougher and tougher to stay focused and stop himself from telling her anything she wanted to know.

Which would be a bad move for a number of reasons. He didn't talk about his past with the women he dated and confiding in Maddy would be more risky than most.

Even after their short acquaintance, he'd figured out that Maddy Westmore was a nurturer at heart. A romantic, despite the rubbish her parents had put her through. Which meant she'd be bound to put her own sentimental spin on whatever he said—and maybe even confuse an urge to confide with an urge to commit. And no way did he want her getting that impression.

But, as Maddy pulled a brass saucepan out of the cabinet, he couldn't deny how good it felt to see her cooking him a meal in the Manor's kitchen. She made the place feel warm.

She looked over her shoulder and smiled. 'Why don't you shower while I cook? It won't take long.' Her eyes sparkled with mischief. 'Unless you want me to scrub your back?'

He coughed and rubbed his thigh. 'Probably not a good idea if we want to eat before midnight.'

She gave an infectious laugh while hefting the saucepan to the sink. Then bent forward to turn on the tap. The purple lace string winked at him again.

Damn. Definitely a thong.

Wrenching his gaze away, he headed for the bedroom.

Better make that a cold shower. Maddy seemed different this evening, determined, somehow—and even more irresistible than usual. He had to keep his wits about him.

For as long as was humanly possible.

'That was sensational.' Rye leaned forward to lift Maddy's hand off the table, his eyes heating as he kissed her knuckles. 'Now, what was that you said about dessert?'

The man looked relaxed and well fed and horny, Maddy thought as her heartbeat pummelled. Mission accomplished. She'd been flirting mercilessly with him all through the meal.

Slipping her hand out of his, she got out of her chair and sat in his lap. 'I have chocolate sauce,' she purred, draping her arms over his shoulders.

He gripped her waist, shifted her weight onto his good thigh. 'Chocolate sauce but no ice cream?'

She giggled. From the prominent bulge pressing into her bottom, she knew she had him. 'We're not going to need the ice cream.'

He cursed softly, humour twinkling in his eyes. 'Are you trying to kill me?'

'How did you guess?'

It was now or never. She'd never seen him so open or so pliable before.

He tugged her closer to nuzzle her neck, but she pressed a finger to his lips. 'Not so fast, King. The chocolate sauce comes at a price.'

He nipped her fingertip, his gaze so hot she could feel her skin sizzling. 'Name it.'

'Tell me why you hate this house so much?' she asked, keeping a stranglehold on her own hormones.

'What?' He barked out a laugh. 'Are you serious?'

'Absolutely.'

'Why on earth do you want to know that?' He didn't sound wary, just astonished. Astonished was good. It would keep his guard down. And she'd already satisfied some of her curiosity. He hadn't denied it. He did hate the house, but why?

'I'm nosy,' she said.

'I noticed.'

'Answer the question, King, or there'll be no chocolate sauce with your dessert.'

He gave his head a shake, looking impressed. 'You are unbeliev…'

'Stop whining and 'fess up,' she interrupted, lazily caressing the curls at his nape. 'I have you at my mercy.'

He let out an exasperated chuckle. 'All right. Fine.' He jostled her on his lap, hot hands stroking under her camisole. 'I'll answer the damn question. But, I warn you, this line of conversation has the potential to turn into a passion killer.'

'I happen to know it would take a nuclear war to kill your passion,' she teased, excitement coursing through her.

He was finally going to let her in; the shutters hadn't come down—and he seemed unable to make them. The surge of pleasure at the thought was almost as potent as the shiver of desire rippling up from her core.

'I hate this house because it's my grandfather's. He didn't want me here. And he made sure I knew it. And the loneliness stuck, I guess.' He said the words easily, with none of his usual caution. A boyish smile edged his lips. 'Until now.'

The second the words slipped out, Rye tensed.

Maddy beamed—as if she were a Sunday School teacher and he a five-year-old who'd just mastered his catechism.

'Oh, Rye,' she whispered, her expression brimming with sympathy and understanding and something that looked disturbingly like tenderness.

Oh, crap. What the hell had he said?

He'd been clinging onto his wits all damn evening with the desperation of a drowning man. While he'd watched her hips jiggle as she'd minced garlic and simmered spices. Through the breathy laugh as she'd whisked their meal onto the table with a flourish. During the slow-motion sweep of her tongue when she licked tomato juice off her full bottom lip. Even when she'd sat on his lap and done that torturous little wiggle. But he'd lost it completely somewhere around the mention of chocolate sauce. He scrambled frantically to get it back.

She stroked his cheek with an open palm, sent him a soft, sexy and unbearably sweet smile. 'Why was it so hard for you to tell me that?'

He jerked his head back, grasped her wrist to hold her hand away from his face. 'Don't!'

'Don't what?' He saw the flicker of hurt, of distress, and loosened his grip.

Calm down. Don't overreact. You've already made an ass of yourself.

'Don't look at me like that,' he said carefully. 'It's not what you're thinking.'

'What am I thinking?' she asked gently.

Yeah, like he was going to step into that minefield.

'Doesn't matter,' he lied, cradling her head in his hand. 'The only thing that matters is this.'

Fisting his fingers in her hair, he captured her mouth. She gave a shocked little sob, but her lips parted. Their tongues tangled, duelled and then danced as she surrendered, her hunger matching his own. His breath panted out as he broke away, the erection he'd been sporting most of the night surging back to life.

'Let's go to bed,' he said, running his hands up her sides to cup heavy breasts.

It wasn't a question but she nodded, looking dazed.

Ten frantic minutes later, as her cries of fulfilment echoed like thunder in his ears, he couldn't drown out one disturbing thought.

How come, the more of her he had, the more he seemed to need?

CHAPTER FOURTEEN

MADDY'S eyes opened and focused on an empty pillow. Which she didn't recognise.

She jerked upright, clasping the fine linen sheet to tender breasts and blinked at the brittle autumnal light seeping through heavy velvet curtains. Pushing her hair out of her eyes, she took in the ornate Victorian furniture, the antique silk rug on polished wood flooring.

Rye's bedroom.

A sigh of distress eased out as the disturbing memories of the night before came tumbling back.

The flirting, the teasing, the dark thrill of desire, the giddy buzz of anticipation. And then the throb of emotion closing her throat and the sting of tears as she had glimpsed something she was never meant to see.

What had she been thinking last night? Why had she been so determined to find out more about Rye, to get to know him better? This was a casual fling. And yet something had changed yesterday. Something that shouldn't have changed. All because of her smug, stupid determination to trick Rye into talking about his past.

She shook her head, trying to forget the bitter humour in his voice when he'd told her about his grandfather. And she'd clearly seen the lost, lonely, traumatised boy he'd been.

Slinging back the quilt, she climbed out of the big bed.

Don't do this, Maddy. Do not do this. He's not a little boy; he's a grown man.

He'd proven that pretty conclusively when he'd taken her to bed afterwards. As for that strange connection she'd felt as they'd made love? A figment of her overdeveloped Miss Fixit gene. It had to be.

Rye King did not need her to heal him, or to look after him. Or to rescue him. He'd made that pretty clear too from the closed off look on his face when she'd clumsily tried to offer comfort.

She dashed around the room, gathering her clothes up off the floor.

Wasn't this what she had always done in the past—believed guys needed her and then got herself trodden all over for her pains? She wriggled into the figure-hugging jeans, pulled her camisole on and finger-combed her hair. She was supposed to be breaking the pattern with Rye, not reinforcing it.

She tiptoed down the hallway to collect her jacket from the kitchen, careful not to look at the remnants of their meal.

As she approached the front door, she heard the low murmur of Rye's voice coming from his office. He was probably busy with his conference call. She should give him a quick wave and then leave. And would act natural while she was doing it if it killed her.

Practical and pragmatic. Confident and independent. That was the new Maddy Westmore. Not some silly twit who had got herself into an emotional pickle of her own making.

She edged the office door open and spotted Rye standing with his back to her, the speaker phone on the desk. His stance was stiff and unyielding, his broad shoulders tense and his hands buried in his pockets as he talked to whoever was on the other end of the line. She hesitated, not wanting to disturb him. But not wanting to leave without saying goodbye. It would look suspicious. She didn't want him to know last night had rattled her—she firmed her chin—even a little.

'I can get over to California next week,' Rye said curtly to his acting CEO John Clements, the thought not appealing to him one bit.

Over the past fortnight he'd been building up his involvement in the business again. Had realised how much he'd missed the daily challenges, the make-or-break decisions, the thrill of being in charge of a business he'd built and watched grow from the ground up. No wonder he'd been in the doldrums after the accident. He'd let so much of what was important in his life slide while he'd been licking his wounds. But as much as he'd enjoyed getting back into the thick of things again, he had no desire to resume the punishing travel schedule that had once been such a huge part of his working life.

'I can check the operation out at The Grange myself,' he continued, knowing it was the only solution that made sense. 'Last time I spoke to Zack, though, he didn't seem nearly as concerned as you are about performance.'

'With all due respect, Mr King,' Clements said in an ingratiating voice, 'that was over six months ago, and the King Xtreme franchise at Mr Boudreaux's resort hasn't reached the projections we were all hoping for in its first year.'

'Which is why I'm flying thousands of miles to sort it out,' Rye snapped.

He eased out a breath. He was tired; he'd been up half the night, unable to sleep, feeling oddly unsettled as Maddy's soft, warm body snuggled against him in the old bed.

'Will you be returning to London after the California trip?' Clements asked.

He ploughed his fingers through his hair. London. Yet another decision he didn't want to think about this morning. 'Probably.' He couldn't hold his return off much longer. 'I'm fully recovered now.' Or as recovered as he would ever be. 'There's nothing keeping me here.' Or nothing he shouldn't be able to handle, he reminded himself.

He ended the call to Clements, feeling dispirited. The faint tap had him swinging round.

'Hi, sorry to bother you.' Maddy stood in the doorway, looking rumpled and sexy in last night's jeans and vest, her face pale.

A surge of longing hit him. He shoved his hands back into his pockets.

For God's sake, King, isn't it about time you put a chokehold on your appetite?

'Hi, you didn't bother me,' he said.

Although she did. He'd been having regular sex—make that non-stop sex—for sixteen days on the trot now. But he couldn't seem to stop behaving like a hormonally charged adolescent boy whenever she was around.

'Um, I should shoot off.' She took a step back, jerked her thumb over her shoulder. 'My shift at the café starts in a couple of hours. I need to shower and change.'

Shower here. With me.

He clamped down on the thought. Stopped himself from asking. Maddy was proving to be more of a distraction than he had anticipated. Last night was proof of that. He still couldn't believe he'd let her seduce him into telling her things he'd never told anyone.

Time to stop letting his libido take charge. 'Okay. Thanks for dinner last night.' He paused, forced the words out. 'I probably won't make it over tonight.'

She nodded, an unusually bright smile on her face. 'No problem.'

And with that she was gone.

He listened to the muffled thump as the front door closed behind her. Glancing towards the window, he resolutely resisted the urge to cross the room and look through the curtains.

Things had got way too intense last night. And he suspected she knew it too, from that stilted and unbearably polite conversation. A night apart would do them both good. They needed a cooling off period.

He had at least a week before he had to make the trip to California, by which time he planned to be ready to cut any lingering ties to Cornwall.

CHAPTER FIFTEEN

'So WHAT are you conjuring up tonight?' Rye's arms circled Maddy's midriff as he whispered the question in her ear.

She smiled, and tried to concentrate on the feel of his warm body against her back. 'Comfort food with a hint of spice.'

She looked out of the window above the sink into the gathering gloom. December was just around the corner. Summer, or rather the miserable excuse for one they'd had this year, was now barely a memory. The cottage's garden had lost all its blooms and the café would be closing in less than a week. Which meant she had to start scouring the classified ads and find another job to tide her over until spring. And stop wasting time mooning over Rye and their non-existent relationship.

'Well, it smells fantastic,' he said, giving her a final squeeze as he let her go. 'I'll set the table; I'm famished.'

'Aren't you always?' she teased with a lightness she was finding it harder and harder to feel.

Their affair would be over soon. It had always been understood. She'd learned her lesson after that night at the Manor and had been careful not to pry since. But she couldn't quite quell the silly fantasy that he needed her. Even though he'd made it blatantly obvious he didn't.

It had been over a week and he still hadn't mentioned the trip to California she'd overheard him arranging. And try as she might not to let his silence bother her, it did. His reluctance to share the information with her had forced her to accept how little she meant to him. And that hurt. Even though she knew it shouldn't.

She watched him bend over her kitchen drawer, his golden hair flopping over his brow as he rummaged for the correct cutlery, and bit back a sigh.

Snap out of it, silly. This is how it has to be. This is what you wanted. No strings. No promises. No one gets hurt.

As she listened to him laying the table in the sitting room and heard the pop of a cork as he opened the bottle of Chablis he'd brought, Maddy busied herself in the kitchen, steaming the chard he'd picked up at the farmer's market and ladling the risotto onto the plates she'd had warming in the oven.

It was just the sex, she thought determinedly as they sat down and she watched him eat her food with his usual enthusiasm. And the company. Also, it had been nice to have someone to cook for who appreciated it. Steve had had a list of food allergies that seemed to multiply every time she tried something new. She adored cooking for Rye. Because he devoured her food with the same enthusiasm as he devoured her body.

And then there was the routine they'd established. It made them seem like a real couple when they never had been.

She stared back down at her plate, pushed the fragrant food around with her fork. This odd sense of regret, of impending loss, couldn't be anything more than endorphins and habit. She'd been repeating the mantra to herself for over a week now. Why couldn't she make herself believe it?

She heard the clink of his knife and fork on her grandmother's china and looked up to find his mesmerising blue eyes fixed on her face. 'Maddy, I have something to tell you.'

'Oh?' she said dully, her mood plummeting. She'd known this was coming; why wasn't she better prepared for it? 'What is it?'

'I have to go to California on a business trip.'

'I know,' she replied, deciding it would be silly to pretend she didn't.

His brow creased. 'You do?'

'Yes, I heard you arranging it. That morning at the Manor.'

'I see,' he said. He seemed momentarily disconcerted by the news, but nothing else. There was no trace of guilt. No sign that he felt she might have been entitled to know his plans a bit sooner. The realisation made the silly spurt of hurt worse.

'We opened a new surf shop and academy at a luxury resort in Big Sur a year and a half ago. I have to go check it out. It's unavoidable, I'm afraid.'

She couldn't quite process what he was saying, the pump of blood in her ears deafening. What was wrong with her? This was ludicrous. She was overreacting, she knew that, but the panic clawed at her chest and chased her heart into her throat.

She forced the question out—the question she'd been trying not to ask even herself in the last week. 'Will you be coming back? To Cornwall?'

'I'm not sure,' he said. 'I haven't decided yet. But I'd like you to come with me to California.'

It took a few frantic moments for her to hear the words properly. Relief came first, coursing through her veins. And then her heart soared as if it were about to burst. He wanted to take her with him? She'd never even considered that as a possibility in the last week.

Holding her hand, he stood up and tugged her out of the chair. His hands settled on her hips. 'The resort's incredible. Belongs to a friend of mine called Zack Boudreaux. I looked at the weather forecast and they're having an Indian summer. Temps in the low seventies. With a couple of wetsuits we could swim in the Ocean, then warm up in the hot tub afterwards.'

It sounded wonderful. Like a romantic fantasy. She could already picture them there together. The dramatic Californian coastline. His gorgeous body, naked and available, driving her to even greater heights of fulfilment. And all the excitement, the passion that had become an integral part of her life since she'd met him. But what seduced her more than that erotic vision was the thought of being there with him. As a real girlfriend. A real companion.

The yearning hit her like a bolt of lightning.

'So what do you say?' He gave her hips a little jiggle, his smile so tempting her heart imploded.

She searched his face, saw not just desire but the complete conviction that she would say yes. And the joyous acceptance that wanted to burst out of her mouth got stuck in her throat. 'I don't think I can.'

His smile faltered. 'You're kidding? Why not?'

She stepped away from him, rubbed her palms up arms which were chilled, despite the heat of the open fire in the hearth. 'Phil's closing the café next week; I have to look for a winter job.'

'So look for a job when you get back.' He sounded more perplexed than annoyed, but still she felt the prickle of temper. She'd never asked him for a thing. Not once. Because she'd thought that was what she wanted. But the offhand offer, which had meant so much to her—and, she suspected, meant very little to him—had made her realise that he'd had every ounce of power in their relationship—however fleeting it was—and she'd had none.

'Why do you want me to come, Rye?'

Rye felt the twin kicks of frustration and confusion.

What did she expect him to say?

That, as the time had drawn near to take the trip, the thought of going had appealed to him less and less. Until he'd figured out what the problem was. He didn't want to go without her.

Of course, the minute he'd realised he wasn't ready to leave her, the thought had annoyed the hell out of him. Had he got suckered into depending on her somehow?

'I'd say it's fairly obvious why I want you along.' He raked his fingers through his hair.

No way was he telling Maddy how he'd agonised over taking the trip without her and then hedged for days about inviting her along. Any feelings he had for her were temporary. He'd made a major mistake by revealing too much the night she had come to the Manor; he wasn't about to make the same mistake again.

'I've been putting the trip off for a while,' he said. 'Because I wasn't looking forward to it. Plane travel will probably aggravate my leg.'

It wasn't true. He'd started doing the exercises the physiotherapist had given him not long after he'd first met Maddy—and he'd noticed the difference instantly. The cramps and muscle spasms had stopped altogether and the tired aching pains that he'd endured almost constantly for months only ever happened now if he'd been on his feet for hours. He'd never be able to surf again, and that still hurt, but the ungainly limp was a lot more manageable and didn't bother him as much any more.

Maddy had never once made an issue of it. In fact, she seemed oblivious to his disability. And, as a result, he'd almost become oblivious to it too. But that didn't stop him from using it as a convenient excuse. 'But then I figured if I mixed business with pleasure it would be less of an ordeal.'

'Well, that's flattering. So I'd be going along to take your mind off things. Is that the idea?' Despite the accusation in her voice, he could see the hurt in her eyes.

He flinched, tried not to let the guilt affect him. He'd made her a promise—that he'd never pretend this was more than it was. All he was doing was keeping that promise. She'd wanted their affair to remain casual as much as he had, so he had nothing to feel guilty about.

'If you don't want to come, all you have to do is say so,' he said, keeping his voice light and non-committal. 'The invitation wasn't meant as an insult.'

But he had insulted her—he could see that too—and he didn't appreciate the renewed stab of guilt one bit.

Her spine straightened and she crossed her arms over her chest. 'I'm sorry. I didn't mean to sound ungrateful.' The fixed smile on her face belied the swirl of emotion in her eyes. 'It was nice of you to offer,' she said, but he could hear the refusal in her voice and an unreasonable anger swelled in his chest.

She wasn't going to come. Why the hell did that bother him so much?

'But I really need to find a job,' she finished.

'Fine, suit yourself,' he said tightly. If she didn't want to come, he wasn't about to beg. However much he might want to.

She bent to stack the plates but he grasped her wrist, pulled her upright. 'Leave them; I'll get them later.'

Wrapping his arm round her hips, he brought her flush against him. 'Let's make up for lost time before I go?'

He clasped her head in his hands, the elemental desire to claim her turning the kiss from chaste to demanding in a heartbeat. But, as he sank his tongue into her mouth, determined to quell the heat pumping into his groin in the only way he knew how, she struggled out of his arms.

'I'd rather not tonight,' she said, the words coming out on a shaky breath. 'I'm tired.'

She was lying. Her pupils had dilated, turning the vivid green of her irises black with desire and her nipples were clearly visible through the thin cotton T-shirt.

He knew exactly how to touch her, how to caress her to make her admit the lie. But he kept his hands rigidly by his sides.

'Fair enough,' he said, the words tasting bitter on his tongue. He cupped her cheek, forced himself to place a friendly kiss on her forehead. 'I'd better be going. Good luck with the job hunt.'

Gathering every last ounce of his willpower, he grabbed his jacket and walked out—and didn't look back.

Maddy watched the pale moonlight gild the bare trees outside her bedroom window and fought back the foolish sting of tears.

The silence in the small cottage seemed suffocating without the comforting rasp of Rye's breathing beside her, or the feel of his rough possessive hand resting on her hip.

Her heart squeezed in her chest. And a lone tear fell. She brushed it hastily aside.

Stop being ridiculous.

She'd done the right thing by turning down his invitation to California, and turning him away tonight.

There's nothing keeping me here.

That was what he'd said to his colleague a week ago. She'd tried to make herself forget the painful little jolt when she'd heard him say it. But the truth was, try as she might, she hadn't been able to.

She couldn't go to California with him, she had to start creating some distance between them, not storing up the sort of lifelong memories that would make him even harder to forget. And sleeping alone tonight was the first crucial step towards regaining her independence.

But, as she drifted into a fitful sleep, the silence wrapped around her like a shroud.

CHAPTER SIXTEEN

'ABOUT damn time you turned up, man.' Zack Boudreaux clapped Rye on the shoulder, then pulled him into a one-armed hug. 'What kept you so long? We haven't seen you in over a year.'

'The slight matter of a bike pile-up and three months in hospital,' Rye replied dryly as his friend released him.

'Yeah, right, heard about that,' Zack said, apparently not the least embarrassed by the gaffe. 'But that was months ago. I happen to know 'cos we sent you…' he paused for a second '…something.'

Rye laughed, grateful to see not a trace of pity or discomfort on Zack's face. 'You mean Kate sent me something,' he shot back, mentioning Zack's wife of four years.

'Kate. Me. Same difference. The point is, you waited six months to come and thank us for it. Whatever it was.' Sitting in one of the armchairs beside the French windows that looked out onto the resort's cliff-top gardens, Zack motioned towards the armchair opposite. 'So maybe you'd like to explain that. Kate was pretty hurt.'

'No, she wasn't.' Rye eased himself into the chair and rubbed his leg. His thigh had stiffened up, thanks to an eleven-hour flight which, even in a First Class bed, had felt a lot longer than before, and the two-hour drive down Highway One to get to the resort. 'I happen to know your wife is made of sterner stuff than that. She's put up with you for four years.'

'Can I help it if the woman's crazy about me?' Despite the humour in Zack's voice, Rye felt a funny little stab of envy.

Weird? While he'd always admired the constancy and companionship Zack and his wife shared, he'd never wanted the same thing for himself. A marriage like theirs required promises he wasn't interested in making, to any woman.

'And don't change the subject, pal.' Zack slung his ankle over his knee, his smile flattening. 'What took you so long?' He pinned Rye with a hard stare. 'I called you, emailed, countless times. Even had to speak to that dumb jerk, Clements. You dropped right off the face of the earth. What the hell happened to you?'

Rye simply stared, stunned by Zack's outburst and the emotion in his friend's voice. The sudden surge of guilt had blood rising up his neck. It had never even occurred to him how his self-imposed purgatory in the last few months might have affected his friends. And Zack was a guy who knew him better than most.

They'd met years before in Vegas, when he'd made the mistake of trying to hustle Zack at the poker table. Zack had bluffed him out of every last penny, but somehow they'd connected. One debauched night at the Bellagio later and they'd been nursing the world's worst hangover together and telling each other their life stories.

He knew Zack and Kate hadn't just sent flowers to his hospital bed. Zack had tried to contact him but he'd refused to communicate with anyone, busy wallowing in his self-pity, and this was the result. He'd managed to upset one of the few people in his life who mattered.

'I didn't know you cared,' Rye said, the lame joke a desperate attempt to cut through the tension.

Zack swore under his breath. Scraping his fingers through his hair, he sent Rye a weak smile. 'Kate's going to kill me. She told me not to lay it all on you the minute you walked in the door. I'm sorry.'

'That's okay. Seems I'm the one who should be sorry,' he said, the guilt intensifying.

Zack huffed out a breath, the smile dying. 'Why did you leave Clements in charge, Rye? Why put some bean-counter in charge of a business you've spent years pouring your life into?'

'Good question,' Rye said, and one he had no answer for any more. 'Don't worry; Clements's days are over. As soon as I get back to the UK, I'll be moving back to London, taking over the reins full-time.'

The statement brought with it a sense of rightness, but also triggered the picture of Maddy that had been lodged in his brain ever since he'd walked away from her two days ago.

He hadn't bothered to contact her since, hadn't even told her that he'd left for California. He didn't have to answer to her; that was already understood. But, more than that, he hadn't wanted to risk a repeat performance of the foolish way he'd behaved that night, when she'd turned down the chance to come with him. He'd convinced himself that his anger, that curious desire to claim her, had been nothing more than hurt pride.

But pictures of Maddy had been crowding into his head ever since. Her bright emerald eyes glinting with pleasure when he teased her. Her wayward curls mussed around her head first thing in the morning when she cooked them breakfast. Her reddened nipples, stung by his stubble, peeking over the quilt as she slept. Even the blush of colour on her cheeks when she told him she didn't want to sleep with him. The memories were so damn vivid they even came with her scent attached, that intoxicating mix of herbs and spices and summer flowers. He damped down the instant surge of reaction, struggled to dismiss the thought.

He wasn't through with Maddy yet; that much was obvious. And that was a problem—one he hadn't figured out yet. But he would. Although he'd have to figure it out sooner rather than later, now he'd committed to returning to London.

'Rye, you scared me, man,' Zack said, accusation heavy in his voice. 'I knew the accident was bad, but when you wouldn't return my calls, when you put that jerk in charge, I figured you'd damaged a lot more than just your leg.'

I did, but it's not damaged any more.

'Truth is, Zack,' Rye said carefully, 'I went a little crazy there for a while.' More than a little crazy. 'In the last few weeks, though, I've come to my senses.'

'Well, good,' Zack said, his smile returning. 'If you don't mind me asking, what turned you around? Six months is a long time to cry over spilt milk.'

Rye chuckled. Zack's offhand assessment of what had been one of the most difficult periods of his life seemed oddly appropriate. 'I met someone,' he said without thinking. 'She made me realise I hadn't lost as much as I thought.'

'Oh, she did, did she?' Zack's eyebrows winged up. 'So the Playboy of the Western World finally got snared.'

'Don't be daft.' Rye backtracked furiously as clammy sweat pooled under his arms.

Maddy was a problem. No question. But that would be a catastrophe.

'It's not like that,' he said emphatically.

'Who are you trying to convince here, buddy?' Zack coughed out another laugh. 'Me or yourself?'

Zack had always had a cruel sense of humour. But Rye couldn't see the joke as the old scars that had festered inside him ever since he'd been twelve opened like a fresh wound.

He didn't feel like that about Maddy—or anyone—and he never would. Because he knew what the consequences were. To love someone, you had to depend on them, to trust them to be there for you when you needed them. And he was never falling into that trap again.

Maybe Maddy had got under his defences, had become an addiction which he was finding it hard to break. But there was nothing more to it than that.

CHAPTER SEVENTEEN

'YOU'RE absolutely positive? You don't have anything?' Maddy's fingers squeezed the mobile. 'I've got a lot of experience and I can provide excellent references.'

The woman on the other end of the phone, the last employer on the list she'd jotted down from the Internet last night, apologised again and hung up.

Maddy dropped the phone into her apron pocket. She'd lost count of how many people she'd rung in the last week, begging for a job. But all the winter work had been snapped up ages ago.

'Still no luck on the job front, eh?' Phil placed two frothy cappuccinos on her tray.

She shook her head, tried not to look as dejected as she felt. She should never have indulged herself with Rye for so long, that much was obvious. She wiped the thought. She couldn't think about him now. He'd been away for over a week and she was in a worse state now than when he'd left.

She'd spent that first day, her day off, scrubbing the cottage until her fingers had been raw. She'd washed the floors, scoured the hob, cleaned out the kitchen cupboards, reorganised her wardrobe and laundered all the bedding in a vain attempt to put him out of her mind, but it hadn't worked. The empty feeling inside her, the aching sadness when she had to cook alone, the well of tears that caught her unawares hadn't gone away. But worse had been the nights and those wildly erotic dreams which woke her in a cold sweat, every cell in her body throbbing, the phantom scent of his skin and the need to have his arms around her so strong the loss felt like a physical blow.

This wasn't how it was supposed to be. She'd never been the clingy type. She had to stop obsessing about this. She'd already decided that if Rye returned she would have to be firm and tell him their affair was over. She couldn't go through all this a second time. A clean break would be best, for both of them. But as hard as that was to contemplate, even harder was the creeping suspicion that Rye had decided not to return to Cornwall after all.

Her bottom lip quivered and she bit into it. Balancing the tray on her arm, she squared her shoulders. 'I'm sure something will come up.'

Phil laid a hand on her shoulder. 'Hey, Mads.' His brows drew together. 'Are you about to cry?'

'No, of course not.' She tried to tug away but he held her easily, plucked the tray off her arm.

'Sit down.' He studied her face as he nudged her onto one of the bar stools. 'And stay put; I'll take these over. Then we're going to have a little chat.'

He was back before she had a chance to do more than sigh. 'Did you ask Rye about working at the hotel? Lover boy owns the place; the least he could do is get you a job.'

'No, I didn't,' she said, folding her arms over her chest. The last thing she needed right now was to be interrogated by Phil. 'He's away.'

'Where is he?'

'California,' she replied curtly. She really didn't want to be talking about Rye. And she absolutely refused to start whimpering in front of Phil.

'For how long?'

'I have no idea.' She threw her hands up, exasperated. 'And, as we're not seeing each other any more—' she paused, swallowing to shift the idiotic constriction in her throat '—I don't really care.' She tried to climb down from the stool, but Phil took her upper arm.

'You guys broke up? Since when?' he asked.

She huffed out a frustrated breath. Why couldn't he let this go? 'We didn't break up. We were never together. It wasn't that sort of thing.'

Phil swore. 'So what sort of thing was it?' The incredulity and annoyance in Phil's tone brought a cold rush of shame. Why did their affair suddenly sound so compromising?

'He was here every damn night behaving as if he owned you,' Phil continued. 'And now suddenly he's gone? I knew he'd do this. That son of a...'

'Phil, I know you mean well,' she interrupted, tugging her elbow out of his grasp, 'but this really isn't any of your business.' She climbed off the stool.

'It is my business when you look dead on your feet and on the verge of tears and one of my friends is the cause.'

'You're not responsible for me,' she said, her spine straightening and the tears drying in her throat.

She'd been a total wimp. And more of a pushover than she ever wanted to admit. But she'd made the decision to have a no-strings affair. And it was her own fault the strings had ended up strangling her. It was way past time to cut loose. 'And neither is Rye. I'm responsible for myself.' Pulling her pencil out of her apron, she shoved it behind her ear. 'Now, I've got a shift to finish, if you don't mind.'

She marched off, her head held high and her back ramrod straight, ignoring the panic that had been clutching at her throat ever since she'd watched Rye walk away a week ago.

She needed to take control of her life again—a control she now realised she'd ceded to Rye, and her hormones, over the last month.

No more avoidance. No more self-indulgence. Today had officially become Pull Yourself Together Day.

She did remarkably well, considering. She got through the rest of her shift without becoming tearful once. She made another round of calls to prospective employers, but didn't let the round of fresh rejections get to her either. She even managed to eat all of the dinner she'd cooked in the stillness of her silent kitchen.

Or nearly all of it. It wasn't until she was running herself a hot bath, determined to get her first restful night's sleep in over a week, and flung open the bottom cabinet to get the bath salts she kept for a special occasion, that Pull Yourself Together Day fell apart at the seams.

There on the shelf was the spare razor and men's shaving gel Rye had left behind. She stared at them for the longest time, before picking them up and placing them carefully in the bin. But then she caught a whiff of the woodsy scent of pine forests and her legs buckled.

She gripped the basin to stay upright and stared at herself in the mirror, her arms and shoulders screaming with tension, the dark shadows under her eyes almost ghoulish.

What was happening to her? How had cool, calm, sensible Maddy turned into a basket case? And why had Rye, of all men, been the trigger? A man who knew her body better than she knew it herself, but cared so little for her he hadn't even bothered to contact her since saying goodbye?

She drew a jerky breath.

Face it; he's not coming back.

She frowned at her bloodshot eyes. She couldn't even cry, the huge black hole opening up inside her making her feel as if she were totally numb and disconnected from reality.

She slumped back down on the toilet seat, pressed her knees together to stop them shaking.

Stop it. It's over and there's nothing you can do about it.

She grabbed some toilet paper, blew her nose, her hands shaking. She'd foolishly believed she was immune to love. And she'd found out in the most devastating way possible she wasn't.

The misery pressed against her chest, the tears she refused to shed making her throat burn.

Not only had she fallen hopelessly in love for the first time in her life. She'd fallen for a man who didn't feel the same way about her and probably never would.

Because he had sealed off his heart at an early age—and was determined never to expose it again.

CHAPTER EIGHTEEN

'MADDY, it's Rye, how are you?'

Maddy's fingers jerked on the handset at the sound of the rich masculine voice on the other end of the line. 'I'm...' She paused; *fine* seemed like an overstatement. 'I'm okay. Where are you?'

'London. I got back from California last night.'

The stupid bubble of excitement, of anticipation burst. 'Okay.'

This was probably good. Just because she'd had some sort of bizarre mental and emotional meltdown and fallen in love with her no-strings fling didn't mean she should pander to it.

'I won't be coming back to Cornwall,' he continued. 'Not for the foreseeable future.'

'Oh.' The word gushed out as air expelled from her lungs and her heart thumped to a stop.

She felt as if she'd been punched in the stomach—even though she had been expecting the news.

He's not coming back. Our affair is over.

'I would have called sooner,' he continued, talking in that reasonable, matter-of-fact tone as Maddy's insides churned and her heart galloped into overdrive. 'But things have been hectic and I thought it would be easier to contact you once I knew what I was doing.'

'Okay.' She knew she sounded like a moron but she couldn't form a coherent thought, let alone a proper sentence. She wanted to be angry with him for being so calm and unruffled when her life had become an emotional car wreck. But all she felt was numb.

'Listen, Maddy, I can't talk right now. I've got an important board meeting in a few minutes. But I want you to come to London. For Christmas.'

'You want…?' She struggled to register the words. 'But why?'

The sensual rumble of laughter made the hairs on the back of her neck stand up. 'Well, apart from the obvious reason,' he said, the husky tone of voice making her pulse points vibrate, 'I may have found a solution to your employment problem. Phil told me you haven't found a job yet.'

The abrupt change of subject threw her completely. 'You spoke to Phil?'

'That's right.' She heard a rustle of papers and then a female voice said something in the background that she couldn't make out. 'Thanks, Pamela,' he said, his voice muffled, 'I'll be there in five.' More rustling. 'Look, I've got to dash. There's a car picking you up in two hours. The flight from Newquay's at four. And bring some of those silk paintings.'

'But…' Why did she feel as if her head were stuffed to bursting with cotton wool?

He chuckled. 'I'll see you at my place this evening.'

'But I…' the deafening sound of the dialling tone interrupted her question '…don't know where you live,' she finished, to no one in particular.

She placed the phone in its cradle and dropped into an armchair. Her hands began to tremble so hard she had to clasp them between her knees and squeeze.

Should she go? Wouldn't she just be prolonging the agony?

She'd barely slept again last night, feeling shaken and confused and desperately unsure of herself. Everything she'd ever believed about herself, about her outlook on life had proved to be wrong and she didn't know how to make it right again.

But how could she not go? And throw away the one chance to find out whether what she felt for Rye was real?

* * *

'George will escort you up to the penthouse, Miss Westmore.'

Maddy nodded at the uniformed concierge, feeling woefully underdressed in her jeans and second-hand suede jacket. She glanced round the palatial foyer of the Kensington apartment block; the fresh scent of tree sap perfumed the air from the enormous spruce, tastefully decorated with silver bows, taking up one corner of the cavernous space.

When the limo from City Airport had pulled up at the art deco building, she'd thought all the sleek steel and stone made quite a statement amid the rows of quaint Victorian mews cottages. As George, the doorman, walked towards her carrying the battered rucksack he'd lifted out of the limo's trunk, it occurred to Maddy that the statement was Ludicrously Wealthy.

'Is Mr King here?' she asked.

The plump, pretty concierge sent her a polite smile. 'Mr King's due back in half an hour. He said to make yourself at home.'

Maddy glanced round the enormous lobby area. Not much chance of that. With its polished teak wall panelling and luxury leather furniture, the place wasn't exactly homely.

'Can you contact him for me?' she asked, trying not to let her annoyance show. She'd rung his mobile about fifty times in the last four hours and got the busy signal and then been given the runaround by his PA, who had insisted he was in meetings all afternoon.

The concierge's perfectly plucked eyebrows drew together a fraction. 'I'm afraid I can't. I could leave a message with Pamela Martin, his PA, if that would be helpful?'

'That's okay.' Pamela Martin already had about twenty messages, none of which had been returned. 'Please don't bother.'

What was the point in trying to contact him, anyway? She was here now. But she wasn't exactly a happy camper.

Having picked herself up off the floor after his call four hours ago, it had taken Maddy a while to get her mind to engage again but, as soon as it had, irritation had started to bubble.

Irritation which had swiftly turned to annoyance, during her fruitless attempts to call him back. Annoyance had then turned to aggravation when she'd realised that she didn't have a choice. He hadn't given her a choice. Rye King had called the shots and she'd been left trailing in his wake.

Maddy knew she could be too appeasing. Too easy-going. Hence Miss Fixit. Cal had always called it her doormat tendency. But, as she'd stuffed brightly coloured silk into her ratty old rucksack and agonised over what else to pack, her ire, at long last, had been well and truly roused.

And it had stayed that way as she'd sat rigidly in the black Mercedes that had arrived to take her to Newquay Airport and in the sleek First Class cabin as she had flown to City Airport.

Rye had walked out on her without a word eight long days ago. He hadn't contacted her once. He'd tricked her into falling in love with him. And then he'd had the cheek to ring her up, effectively snap his fingers and expect her to jump to attention without a proper explanation.

The assumption that she would be sharing his bed in London only added fuel to the flames of Maddy's temper.

Since when did having a casual fling mean that he got to make all the decisions and she was just supposed to step into line? Fortunately, stewing in her own anger and frustration had a hefty fringe benefit. As long as she was concentrating on how mad she was with him, she didn't have to dwell on the much bigger problem—what on earth she was going to do about the fact that she'd fallen in love with him?

As George directed her into the panelled lift and closed the ornate cage doors with a creak, Maddy tried not to be intimidated. She resolutely refused to be overwhelmed in any way by the trappings of Rye's wealth. She had more than enough to worry about without letting his snazzy home bother her too.

Then the lift jolted to a stop and George opened the doors onto a marbled lobby area. Maddy's boot heels clicked on the tiles. Large bunches of red lilies stood in black onyx vases, decorating the lavish space. She stopped and gawped, dropping her head back to see the lights of a passing plane blinking through the domed glass atrium above her head.

Maddy sucked in a breath. Okay, this was more than just snazzy. This was an alternative reality.

Depositing her rucksack on the cool marble floor, George gave a gallant little bow and left.

As the lift doors clanked closed, Maddy ventured into the apartment proper. Thick royal-blue carpets accented off-white walls hung with an array of modern art in the main hallway. Maddy's mouth formed an O as she recognised some of the artwork and realised they were originals. She hurried past a series of doors, then stopped dead at the end of the corridor. With a double-height ceiling and one whole wall devoted to a panoramic view of Kensington Gardens, the penthouse's main living space was breathtaking.

The minimalist decor, which was both tasteful and unobtrusive, had obviously been coordinated by a professional decorator. She couldn't see Rye bothering to hunt up a rug edged with the exact same shade of turquoise as the waist-high glass brick wall that separated the lavish living area from the state-of-the-art kitchen. Or spending hours decorating the Christmas tree in one corner with pinpoint lights and colour-coordinated red and gold ornaments.

Spotting a console embedded into the wall with loads of dials and displays, she wondered if it was for the inbuilt sound system or the huge plasma TV over the fireplace.

She sighed. Probably both.

She stood, her reflection dwarfed by the windows that looked out over a decked balcony. This was the lavish bachelor pad she'd expected Rye to have all those weeks ago, before she'd got to know him, with its new-fangled boy toys and expertly coordinated interior design.

But how could the man she had come to know since live in a place like this? It was as if Rye King were two different people. The urbane billionaire businessman with a swanky penthouse pad in Kensington who probably dined at a new 'in' restaurant every night, and the sexy ex-surfer who was happy to slum it in Cornwall and devoured her home cooking as if he were starving to death.

But which man was the real Rye King? Had she fallen in love with a man who had never really existed?

The soft ping of the lift bell had Maddy freezing in place.

She heard the telltale creak and clatter of the lift doors opening. Uneven steps hit the marble foyer tiles, then became muffled by the thick wool carpet in the hallway.

'Maddy, where are you?'

She wrapped her arms round her midriff. 'In the living room,' she called out, her voice sounding small and fragile.

He walked in, looking tall and dangerous in a steel-grey designer suit. A broad grin spread across his features as his gaze roamed over her figure. 'You came.'

She hugged herself tighter. He sounded like Rye, he even looked like Rye in some ways. The chiselled features, the mischievous sparkle in those pure blue eyes and his uneven gait were still there. But so much else was different. The unruly hair that had always been carelessly tossed back from his brow had been recently cut so it hugged his head in stylish waves. His clean-shaven jaw lacked its usual five o'clock shadow. The expertly tailored suit accentuated his broad shoulders and narrow hips, making him seem taller and even more imposing. And his skin had a light tan, unlike the winter pallor of a week ago.

He was as breathtakingly handsome as she remembered. But somehow a virtual stranger.

'Did I have a choice?' The brittle tone hid the tremor in her voice.

The grin only widened as he crossed to her. He gripped her arms, stroked his thumbs into the curve of her elbows. 'You're angry with me,' he remarked, confident humour in his tone.

She pulled out of his grasp, her temper snapping back to life. 'Funnily enough, yes, I am.'

She turned round, marched to the window. She didn't want to get mad. 'You walk off without a word. You don't call. And then you expect me to come running.' She swung back, glad to have the distance between them. 'I don't appreciate being treated as if I'm your mistress. Because I'm not and I don't want to be.'

He made his way towards her, the confident grin still in place. Cupping her cheek, his warm palm settled on her neck and sent an instant quiver through her. 'So why did you come?'

She opened her mouth, ready to throw the news that she loved him at him. But the words got trapped in her throat. She jerked back, angled her body away so that he couldn't see the vulnerability in her eyes. 'Because, for some stupid reason, I missed you.'

He gave a self-satisfied laugh and her heart squeezed.

'Good.' His thumb stroked down the line of her neck. She felt the warmth of his body as he stepped behind her, settled a hand on her waist. Of its own accord, her body swayed into his. 'Because, for some stupid reason—' he paused, his lips brushing the sensitive skin at her nape '—I missed you too, Maddy.'

Electric jolts shot through her as his lips caressed her neck, but she stiffened, drew away. 'If you missed me you would have called.'

The evidence was irrefutable. As much as she might want it to be true, he hadn't missed her as much as she had missed him.

His arm banded across her midriff, trapping her against him. She felt the heat of his erection against her bottom. 'I say we make love,' he murmured, the feather of his breath brushing her cheek, 'and argue about this later.'

She shoved his arm away, whipped round, anger at herself and her foolish heart making bitter tears spring into her eyes. 'I told you, I'm not your mistress.'

CHAPTER NINETEEN

RYE tried to school his features, tried to wipe the smile off his face, tried to feel guilty about the shimmer of angry tears in her eyes. But the task was next to impossible when he was so overjoyed to see her. And when the unfamiliar show of temper only made her more beautiful.

He hadn't seen her in a snit for a long time, not since their first few days together. She was one of the most even-tempered, easy-going people he'd ever met, settled and content, and it was one of the things he had missed the most in the days they'd been apart. Because it made him feel settled too when he was with her. But, while he hated to be a cliché, the way the unfamiliar spurt of temper lit her eyes and brought vivid colour to her cheeks made her even more adorable. If that were possible.

'Maddy, I don't think of you as my mistress,' he said evenly, not really wanting to placate her, but knowing he should.

'Don't you?' she said, her voice defiant. 'Then why are you treating me like one?'

'I'm not. I wanted you to come to London for a number of reasons.' He thrust his tongue into his cheek to stop from smiling. 'Not *all* of them sexual.'

Her eyes narrowed to slits. 'You actually think this is funny. Don't you?'

He grasped her wrist as she tried to pass him.

'Let go. I'm leaving,' she said, trying to prise his fingers loose.

He drew her rigid body towards him, wrapping his arm around her hips to hold her in place.

'Don't be daft,' he said. 'You didn't come all this way just to walk off in a huff ten minutes after you got here.'

She wriggled furiously, her eyes flashing to his as his growing erection butted against her. 'I didn't come all this way just so you could poke me the minute I got here either.'

He choked back a laugh. 'Fair enough.' He lifted his hands, letting her scramble away. 'How about we call a truce? You don't run off. And I promise not to poke you.' He paused, unable to resist the suggestive grin. 'Yet.'

Temper flared but she schooled it, the flush of colour more vivid. And he felt the first tug of guilt.

She was right. He had been selfish and manipulative. And he knew it. When he'd spoken to her on the phone that morning, he'd heard the shock and the disappointment, then the confusion in her voice and he'd trampled over all three to get what he wanted.

He'd railroaded her into coming, deliberately making himself unavailable so she would find it impossible to back out. He wasn't going to give her a second opportunity to turn him down the way she had a week ago. They needed to get this thing sorted between them once and for all.

He'd given the problem of Maddy Westmore a lot of thought while he was in California and had figured it all out. Maddy wasn't really the issue so much as the circumstances.

She'd caught him at a vulnerable time in his life. The accident had knocked his confidence more than he'd wanted to admit. He'd never originally intended to spend so much time with her, but the evenings they spent together had become like a drug. The cottage, with its worn, comfortable furniture, infused with the scent of herbs and spices and decorated in Maddy's cluttered but welcoming style, had relaxed him, while Maddy's responsive little body and sweet, undemanding companionship had made him feel whole again.

Bringing her to London would help to put that episode of his life behind him once and for all. This was where he belonged, in the cut and thrust of the thriving metropolis. And Maddy didn't. Once they'd burnt out the last of the sexual chemistry they shared, they'd both be ready to go their separate ways with no regrets.

The little trickle of guilt dried up. He wasn't a hypocrite and had always believed the ends justified the means. So, frankly, it was stupid to feel bad about tactics he'd planned so methodically for eleven solid hours on the plane back from California.

Especially when those tactics, however underhand, had produced the desired result. Maddy, in London, in his apartment.

He gave a heavy sigh. Only problem was, if they were going to make productive use of her time here, he'd have to pour some water onto the fire—no matter how tempting it was to watch it spark and sizzle.

He stepped towards her, tucked a forefinger under her chin, brought her gaze to his.

'I don't think of you as my mistress, Maddy. And I didn't bring you here to become my sexual plaything. If you don't want to sleep with me, you certainly don't have to.' Although he'd do his damnedest to make her change her mind.

'That's very noble of you, Rye.' The colour rose even higher in her cheeks. 'When you know perfectly well how hard it is for me to resist you.' She didn't sound pleased but the admission made the heat in his groin pulse harder nonetheless.

'So what's the problem, then?' he asked.

Her gaze fixed on his, the depth of feeling sending a ripple of unease through his arousal.

'This isn't a casual fling any more,' she murmured. 'Not for me. And it hasn't been for a while.' The softly spoken words were followed by a resigned sigh. 'I really did miss you. I missed you a lot. And that scares me.'

The brutal honesty of the statement struck him first. One of the qualities that had endeared her to him right from the start was her refreshing lack of guile. She had no secrets, no subterfuge. Unlike all the other women he'd ever dated. Maybe it was for that reason that he felt the need to be honest back. Surely he owed her that much. He knew that they had no future in the long-term. He would never be able to make the sort of commitment that would lead to the kind of life his friends Zack and Kate led. But Maddy wasn't asking him for that.

'Maddy, I missed you too.' He cupped her cheek, the need to touch her overwhelming him. 'I didn't contact you because I thought it would pass. And it felt like crossing a line I had no right to cross. But it didn't pass. It only got stronger. Which is why I crossed that line and invited you here.' He threaded his fingers into the short cap of hair, rubbed the silky ends between his fingers. 'I can't make any promises. And it wouldn't be fair to you if I did.' He drew a deep breath. 'I've never had a long-term relationship. And I don't want one now. But this isn't casual for me either. Not any more.' He huffed out a strained laugh. 'And if that scares you, believe me, it scares me a lot more.'

The minute he'd made the candid admission he flinched. He sounded like a romantic fool. What was he talking about? This affair wasn't as casual as it had been, but did he really want her to know that?

But then he looked into her face and saw the same uncertainty, the same confusion that he himself was battling and the panic faded. She leant into his palm, covered his hand with hers, the gesture so warm, so giving, so accepting and so like her that the rapid ticks of his heartbeat slowed.

She blinked, the sheen of tears in her eyes dispelled by the quick, flirtatious grin. 'I really hope you're not just saying that to get into my knickers?'

He grinned at her as he touched his forehead to hers and caressed her neck. 'Actually, I didn't. But if I'd known it was going to help get me into your knickers—' he paused to curve his other hand around her lower back and slip his fingers beneath the waistband of her jeans '—I would have said it a lot sooner.'

She laughed as he explored the top swell of her buttocks.

'Talk is cheap,' she said, stretching up to clasp her hands

around his neck, the sinuous movement torturing him. 'I think now action is required.'

He chuckled and pulled her towards him. Slanting his lips across hers, he thrust his tongue into her mouth, giving her the kiss he'd been wanting to give her ever since he'd spotted her in his living room.

It took them less than ten seconds to make it to the nearest bedroom, and only a few seconds more to tear each other's clothes off.

He dragged her onto the bed, rejoicing as he slid his fingers into hot swollen flesh and found her wet and ready.

'Damn. Condoms,' he snarled, gritting his teeth as he tried to keep a stranglehold on the need to bury himself inside her.

'I'll get them. Where are they?' she gasped.

'Bedside table.'

He gave a rough chuckle as she grabbed the protection out of the drawer, obviously as eager as he to consummate the passion that had been building for over a week.

After enduring the exquisite torture while she rolled the latex on with frantic fingers, he gripped her hips and forced her to straddle him. She choked out a sob as she impaled herself on his powerful erection. He delved into the curls at her core and found her clitoris, making her cry out as she rode them both to completion. The tight clasp of her body shot him over the edge in record time as heat exploded in his groin.

Her panting breaths brushed his cheek as she collapsed on top of him, the aftershocks of the brutal climax rippling through his body. His hands skimmed up her back, the musty scents of sex and sweat mingling with the flowery spice of her.

He tucked her hair behind her ear, kissed the lobe as her unsteady breathing slowed.

'It's good to have you back,' he whispered.

He felt the instinctive clench of her body on the still firm erection.

'It's good to be back,' she murmured, her voice groggy with exhaustion.

As she relaxed into sleep, he held her on top of him, prolonging the intimate connection between them a few moments more, and made a promise to himself.

However long it took to work this thing they had together out of their systems, he'd make sure he was careful with her—especially when it was time to let her go.

Maddy awoke with a jolt, her body stiff. Heat pumped off Rye like a furnace and she realised she still lay on top of him, her cheek glued to his chest. She shifted over.

The tingle of shame made it hard for her to give in to sleep as she curled away from him. She should have told him she'd fallen in love with him. Why hadn't she told him?

He grunted, his hand circling her waist as he hauled her back into the curve of his body. ''Sbetter,' he murmured, his nose buried in her hair.

She lay in his arms, happy to be held, the guilt and recriminations fading as she listened to his breathing even back into sleep.

She'd have to tell him eventually. She knew that. But why tell him now? And make things even more complicated than they already were. He hadn't made any commitments—but then neither had she. They were still feeling their way, investigating what they really had together.

She loved him. But did she really know what that meant? Or whether it would last? Maybe her love for Rye was as fickle as her parents' love for each other had been, based on sexual chemistry and little more. Spending time with him in his real life would help answer those questions.

But, even as she drifted off to sleep, trying to remain sensible, her heart skipped at the tantalising prospect that what Rye had told her—about missing her, about being scared too and about not being casual about their affair any more—meant he was falling for her too.

CHAPTER TWENTY

'Wake up, sleepy-head.'

The smell of pine forests and spicy aftershave beckoned Maddy from a deep, dreamless sleep. She stretched, and sighed as Rye's handsome face came into focus.

Then frowned. 'You're dressed?' she murmured, her voice rough with sleep as she took in the pristine white shirt, the maroon silk tie draped round his neck and the sheen of water in his slicked back hair.

His lips curved into a sexy smile and her heart galloped into her throat. 'It's almost midday.' He straightened and flipped up his collar, looped his tie underneath. 'I have a meeting in about…' he glanced at the pricey watch on his wrist. The sterling silver timepiece was one she didn't recognise. 'Damn. Ten minutes.'

She pushed up on her elbows, tucked the sheet under her armpits. 'I'm sorry; you should have woken me.'

'Now she tells me,' he said, giving a soft laugh as he knotted his tie. 'I was being noble.' He looked at her, his smile full of sensual promise. 'I exhausted you last night.'

She coloured slightly, remembering the two times he'd woken her during the night.

He finished with the tie and flipped down his collar. Cradling her cheek, he pressed his lips to hers in a brief possessive kiss. 'And, let me tell you, I deserve a medal for being so restrained.'

She grinned at his playfulness. 'I'll have to reward you later.'

'I'm counting on it.' He stood and grabbed his suit jacket off the bed. 'Listen, there's fresh coffee in the kitchen and some pastries.' He shrugged on the jacket, which draped perfectly over his broad shoulders, then sank a hand into the pocket of his trousers. 'Ring the concierge if there's anything else you want. I haven't got much in the place because I usually skip breakfast.'

She settled back to watch him grab his wallet and keys from the dresser, puzzled by the admission. He'd always devoured a full plate for breakfast, his appetite ravenous in the morning whenever he'd stayed at the cottage.

'I could go shopping and make us dinner?' she said, eager to keep busy during the time without him.

He hesitated for a moment before pulling some notes out of his wallet. 'Don't bother. I thought we could eat out tonight.'

She watched him flip out several notes, trying not to be hurt by the casual rejection of her offer.

'But get whatever else you need,' he said, dropping the money on the dresser.

She bolted upright. 'I have my own money, Rye.'

'I know.' He leant over her to give her a quick peck on the forehead. 'But this area is expensive.'

She could well imagine. 'Even so, I don't need your money.'

'Then don't spend it,' he said, leaving the notes on the dresser. 'I'll send a car this evening. I'm afraid I've got a pretty busy day scheduled so I'll have to meet you at the restaurant. But there's someone I want to introduce you to before we eat.'

'Who?'

He simply grinned. 'I'll explain later. I've got to run.'

And, with one more quick kiss, he was gone.

She huffed out a slow breath, and felt the aching sensation of confusion and uncertainty as she flopped back onto the pillows.

They'd made love three times since she had arrived. The

first time fast and frantic, the second full of heat and passion and the third slow and tender. She could still feel the firmness, the tenderness between her thighs where he had lodged deep inside her. But, as familiar as his body was, and the exhilarating pleasure it could give her, she couldn't shake the feeling that the moody, magnetic man she had fallen hopelessly in love with during those idyllic weeks in Cornwall was only one small facet of Ryan King.

Their relationship didn't feel equal any more. And not just because of his money or his lavish lifestyle. She had no idea how he felt about her.

A vicious shiver racked her body, despite the climate-controlled temperature in the luxurious bedroom.

'Get a grip, woman,' she murmured.

She was getting ahead of herself as usual. She needed to make the most of her time with Rye in London. Get him to open up about how he felt. And she wasn't going to be able to do that if she had a panic attack at the first sign of the unfamiliar. Her time in London was going to be an adventure. And, like all the best adventures, it was as scary as it was exciting.

Swinging her legs to the floor, she stood up and wrapped the sheet around her. She'd have a shower, get her stuff unpacked and then explore the apartment and the neighbourhood beyond, as Rye had suggested.

She studied the bedroom. She'd been too preoccupied last night to take in the splendour of Rye's home properly. With its high ceilings and understated but impossibly chic interior design, the master bedroom had the same take-your-breath-away effect as the living room.

She headed for the en suite bathroom, eager to explore, and spotted the notes he'd left on the dresser. Her brow creased as she tugged the sheet tighter around her breasts.

Rye might not think of her as his mistress, but the blithe way he'd dismissed her objections to the money suggested he was used to being blasé about his wealth, and probably unnecessarily generous with the women he dated.

After the argument they'd had last night about his high-handed attitude, she'd been annoyed by the offer of money. But his attitude was probably as much her fault as his.

Right from the start, he'd made all the decisions in their relationship and she'd let him. Partly because it was in her nature to be non-confrontational. But also because she'd found the forcefulness of Rye's character—his independence, his authority, his desire to take control—extremely attractive, because it was so unlike the other men she'd dated. But she could see now that the same qualities which had made Rye so appealing to begin with could also become an obstacle to their future happiness—if she didn't start standing up to him.

Calling him to task yesterday for his domineering behaviour had been a very good start. But she needed to follow through— opening the top drawer on the dresser, she swept the notes inside and slammed it shut—which meant she wasn't going to let him treat her like his kept woman.

Gripping the sheet in her fists, she headed for the bathroom.

She'd accepted his hospitality but she didn't intend to sit idly in his apartment all day while he went off to work either. The Christmas season was approaching and there were lots of posh shops and cafés round the corner in Kensington High Street that might be looking for casual staff. Why not go exploring and check out her employment prospects while she was at it?

She doubted he'd be too pleased with the idea. But she was not going to be intimidated by Rye's money, or his lavish lifestyle, or the force of his will either—however indomitable. Because she'd recently discovered she had a will of her own. Plus she had something to fight for now that would be worth winning.

Not only Rye's love, but also his respect.

Not being intimidated by Rye and his lifestyle turned out to be a lot easier said than done, Maddy realised, as the maître d' led her through the bijou Notting Hill restaurant he'd booked for dinner. She brushed her palms down the chic midnight-blue cashmere dress she'd splurged on in the hope of finding a job quickly and tried not to worry too much about her fruitless search for employment so far.

It didn't matter; she would try again tomorrow. And the dress had been worth it. She'd rather live on yoghurt for a month than have to walk through a place like this in her old black wraparound or, worse, a T-shirt and jeans.

Glasses and cutlery clinked, conversation dimmed to discreet murmurs, the air redolent with the seductive scent of freshly cut holly, expensive perfume and delicate spices. The cellar restaurant had an exclusive air reinforced by the plush velvet-curtained booths and the number of beautiful people they seemed to number among their clientele. Maddy struggled not to gawp as she was escorted past a table where a supermodel was sharing a candlelit dinner for two with a young rock star who had recently topped the charts.

Yup, the dress had definitely been worth every penny.

'Mr King and Ms Chelmsford are waiting for you in the private annexe,' the Maître d' announced as he whisked open a glass door at the end of the restaurant.

Ms Who?

Maddy blinked as she stepped into what looked like a tropical rainforest, the lush plants in stark contrast to the winter flora that had decorated the rest of the place. She spotted Rye, sitting at the only table, deep in conversation with an impossibly chic middle-aged woman in a tailored trouser suit. He tilted his head back and laughed at something the woman said, the strong column of his throat drawing Maddy's eye. But then his companion bent forward and touched his wrist. Maddy's stomach dipped at the intimacy of the gesture.

The maître d' announced her presence and the woman's fingers drew back as Rye braced his hands on the table to stand up.

'At last, you're here.' His blue eyes lit with appreciation as he crossed towards her and the little dart of jealousy vanished. Grasping her around the waist, he gave her a long, lingering kiss that had heat rising up her neck.

'This is Ruth Chelmsford,' he said, keeping his arm round her waist as he introduced her. 'She's an old friend of mine.'

The woman rose and offered her hand. 'It's lovely to meet you.' Her handshake was firm and friendly and her smile unguarded, making Maddy feel foolish for her suspicions. 'Rye has been talking my ear off about you for twenty minutes.'

'He has?'

The woman laughed easily at Maddy's gauche comment as Rye pulled out a chair for her.

'You look incredible,' he whispered, his breath brushing her nape. 'Relax.'

She settled in the chair and tried to do just that.

'Yes, he has,' Ruth said indulgently. 'Rye thinks you may have something I want,' she continued.

'Here's one of them,' Rye remarked. Then, before Maddy could stop him, he plucked off the silk scarf she had tied round her waist to accent her dress and handed it to Ruth. 'What do you think?'

Ruth held the scarf up by its corners as if it were spun gold. 'It's exquisite.' Her eyes locked on Maddy's as she lowered the scarf to her lap. 'You created this yourself?'

'Yes, I... It's sort of a hobby,' she replied, a little embarrassed by the praise.

'How many of them do you have?'

'I'm not sure.' She glanced at Rye, confused. But all he did was wink at her, confusing her even more. 'Why do you want to know?'

The woman laughed. 'Because I'm the chief buyer for DeMontfort's of Piccadilly. We've been looking for a new silk designer for our spring collection. And I think I may have found her.'

'You mean...?' It was Maddy's turn to gasp. Had this woman called her a designer? 'DeMontfort's? Seriously?'

The exclusive London department store had been a fixture in the West End for over a century. But in the last thirty years it had become a world leader in the fashion world as well, famous for showcasing bold new British design talent. She'd window-shopped there herself the few times she'd visited London, adoring the store's grace and beauty and the innovation of its displays. But she'd never been able to afford any of the merchandise.

'Unfortunately, time is of the essence,' Ruth said, apparently oblivious to Maddy's shocked expression. 'We're launching the spring range with a charity gala at The Savoy on the fifteenth, so I'll need to see whatever you have, select the pieces we can use.'

'How many did you bring with you?' Rye said softly beside her, his hand covering hers and jolting her out of her stupor.

'About…' she paused, tried to think with her head spinning and her heart jumping '…about ten, maybe.'

'Ten is a good start. But we'll need more. Luckily, we have a workshop in Soho with space you can use. We can supply…'

The woman's voice faded into the distance as the drumming of Maddy's heartbeat began to deafen her. She answered the barrage of questions on autopilot, trying to breathe through the knowledge that something she'd never even dreamed of, something she would have been too scared to dream of, was actually happening.

She could make a living out of her silk work? She loved it. Had always loved it. But it had never even occurred to her that it would be good enough to sell. And not just sell. From the snippets of Ruth's conversation she could actually process, it seemed the woman thought she could sell it at a very decent price indeed.

'Ruth, give her a minute, she's not committing to any of that yet.' Rye's sure, certain voice cut through the fog of awe and excitement. 'We'll get the other silk sent over tomorrow morning. When you've drawn up a contract—and I've had my solicitor look at it—and once Maddy's had a chance to digest all this.' Rye's hand squeezed hers on the table. 'Then you can talk to her again and iron out the details.'

Ruth gave an astonished laugh. 'Why, Rye, you sound protective.' She stood up. 'Clearly Maddy here is even more special than I imagined.'

Rye's hand tensed and lifted off hers as Ruth excused herself and left the annexe.

'I can't believe it. DeMontfort's? It's like a dream,' Maddy said, excitement bubbling.

Rye gave a gruff chuckle, the moment of tension gone. 'You deserve it. You've got a rare talent.' Sitting back, he lifted the menu. 'Now, how about we order dinner and a bottle of Dom, then grab a cab back to mine and make wild passionate love for the rest of the night to celebrate?'

Maddy giggled as he wiggled his eyebrows suggestively, feeling young and carefree and so in love she was sure she was about to burst.

How could he have known she wanted this, when she hadn't even known it herself? And how could he have taken the time and trouble to make it happen if he wasn't at least a little bit in love with her too?

Rye listened to Maddy's breathing deepen as she lay exhausted in his arms, his body still humming from the afterglow of their passionate celebration, but his own refused to do the same. Ruth's throwaway comment earlier played over and over again in his mind like a cracked record.

Clearly Maddy here is even more special than I imagined.

Ruth had always been remarkably perceptive. When he'd been a brash young entrepreneur of twenty-five, it was one of the things about her he'd liked the most. She'd been perceptive enough to realise their brief but passionate affair had no future without him having to tell her—and because of that she was one of the few women he'd managed to stay friends with. But the knowledge that she knew him better than most only made her comment all the more disturbing.

Maddy wasn't special. He couldn't let her be. Whatever Zack and now Ruth believed. But even though she wasn't special, she was definitely different.

When had he ever cut a business trip short because he missed a woman so much he couldn't be without her? And when had he ever found it this hard to let one go?

He'd actually been concerned about inviting Maddy to Graystone's for dinner. The restaurant was one of the most sought-after places to eat in London—frequented by the very top echelons of the capital's business and entertainment worlds—and he'd worried about her feeling out of place and uncomfortable. But when she'd walked in, the blue dress clinging to her curves and making his mouth go bone-dry, he was the one who had felt uncomfortable. Because the desire to carry her off and then gobble her up in a few quick greedy bites had been stronger than ever.

Why did she fit here every bit as much as she did in that tiny cottage on the cliffpath? And when was he going to start tiring of her? Because they'd been together for over a month now. Which was already a record for him.

He'd planned the meeting with Ruth with one simple motive in mind. If Ruth liked Maddy's work, it would absolve him of any lingering guilt over their affair. He'd used Maddy to repair his own battered ego and it seemed only fair to give her something back.

But the simple motive had backfired. He'd got a genuine thrill out of Maddy's awestruck expression when Ruth had talked about the DeMontfort's show, and her excited chatter all the way home in the cab about the prospect of her future career—not to mention the heady enthusiasm with which she'd made love to him when they got back to the apartment. She'd looked at him as if he had given her something precious— and made him wish that his motives had been as pure as she believed.

She stirred against him in her sleep, the movement sweet and sexy and so trusting he huffed out a sigh.

He had to reset the boundaries between them.

He took a deep breath of her intoxicating scent.

And somehow find a way to stick to them this time.

CHAPTER TWENTY-ONE

'MADDY, dear—' Ruth peered at her as she poured the pot of tea '—you look exhausted.'

Maddy took the ornate china teacup Ruth offered her and sipped at the delicate brew, trying to mask the creeping fatigue that had begun to sap her strength. 'I'm fine. Really.'

'You're not fine. That much is obvious,' Ruth said, her eyes clouded with sympathy as she draped the designs they had been discussing over her desk. 'Is it the show? I've been working you like a slavedriver.'

Maddy shook her head. 'I'm so excited about tonight, that's all. I'm finding it hard to sleep,' she murmured, fingering the silk, not quite able to look Ruth in the eye.

She put the teacup down carefully on the tray, felt the emotions that had been so close to the surface for two weeks well up inside her. Who was she kidding? Her lack of sleep had nothing to do with the charity gala and everything to do with her relationship with Rye.

At first she'd tried to persuade herself it was her imagination—and the stress caused by the manic preparations for the show. Just because Rye had insisted they go out every single night and seemed reluctant to spend any time alone her. They still made love every evening and often in the morning as well. And he had been a charming and considerate host, planning a series of outings and excursions. He'd taken her ice skating one evening at the rink at Somerset House, bought box seats for a show in Shaftesbury Avenue, wined and dined her in a number of swanky restaurants and nightclubs.

But gradually she'd begun to feel as if the whirlwind of social engagements he kept insisting on were really just more of the diversionary tactics he'd employed so skilfully all along. She'd hoped that their relationship would deepen, strengthen while she was in London but, honestly, the reverse seemed to be happening.

'Does Rye know you're in love with him?'

Maddy's head jerked up at Ruth's softly spoken question. 'I'm sorry—what?' she said, but the flush was already creeping up her neck.

Ruth crossed her legs and smoothed her skirt over her knees. 'You haven't told him, have you, my dear?'

She could try to deny it, but somehow the concern on Ruth's face had the emotion swelling in her throat. She dipped her head, gave it a little shake. 'How did you know?' she asked, twisting her hands together in her lap.

Ruth's hand covered hers and squeezed. 'I recognised the symptoms. Six years ago, I went through the same thing myself. And I'm sure I looked as unhappy and as unsure of myself as you do right now.'

Maddy looked up, the sympathy and total understanding in Ruth's gaze making tears prickle the backs of her eyes. 'You and Rye were lovers?'

Ruth nodded. 'We had a brief fling. As I suspect you guessed when we first met.'

Maddy nodded, desperately embarrassed. She had guessed it, but she'd gone into denial about that as well as everything else in the past few weeks.

'There's no need to feel awkward,' Ruth remarked, sending Maddy a warm smile. 'It only lasted a few weeks. I was forty and had just gone through a particularly bitter divorce when Rye came along. He was fifteen years younger, impossibly gorgeous and devastating in bed—and of course I fell stupidly in love with him. But it meant absolutely nothing to him.'

Delivered in an amused tone, Ruth's candid confession didn't bring on the jealousy Maddy would have expected.

'I'm sorry. Rye didn't say anything,' Maddy murmured.

Ruth patted her hand. 'Of course he didn't. Why would he? Rye left me as soon as he realised I was getting serious about him. And there have been a string of women since, who I've watched go through the same unhappy experience. I'm grateful that we managed to remain friends, but much more grateful that episode of my life is over. Heartache can be hell on the complexion, you know.'

Maddy huffed out a laugh, but her own heart felt as if it were being torn out of her chest, because Ruth's words had brought her face to face with exactly what it was that had been so wrong in the past weeks. Rye had been shutting her out and she'd been too scared to even admit it to herself, let alone confront him about it.

Maddy's palms dampened as her heartbeat began to hammer like a pneumatic drill. She should have told Rye two weeks ago how she felt. She'd promised herself she wouldn't be a push-over any more, that she'd stand up for herself. And she hadn't. Because she'd been scared to risk the sort of confrontation she'd spent her whole life avoiding.

'I have to tell him how I feel,' she murmured.

'I'm afraid so,' Ruth said quietly. 'Rye has a pattern that won't allow him to get close to anyone. And he's far too pig-headed to change it on his own.'

Maddy nodded. She'd suspected as much all along—that he'd never recovered from the loss of his parents and he'd been protecting himself in the only way he knew how ever since.

'But how can I change it, if he won't let me?'

'I've seen the way he looks at you, my dear.' Ruth sent her a reassuring smile. 'I believe you already have.'

CHAPTER TWENTY-TWO

'SUCCESS agrees with you, Maddy. You look gorgeous tonight.' Rye cupped her cheek as he leaned across their table. 'But I'm not waiting much longer to find out what you've got on under that gown.'

Maddy smiled, the familiar flirtation helping to stem the apprehension that had been building inside her ever since her conversation with Ruth that afternoon. 'Ruth promised me she only has one more set of buyers to introduce me to. Then we can make a run for it.'

Hearing the orchestra in the ballroom next door strike up a slow, seductive waltz, her smile became wistful. 'Did you know, we've never danced together,' she murmured before she could think better of it.

Standing up, he tugged her gently out of her chair. 'That's easily remedied.'

She held back. 'Are you sure?' She hadn't meant to pressure him into doing something he wasn't comfortable with. 'What about your leg?'

He sent her a wolfish grin as he led her into the ballroom, which was already crowded with beautiful people dancing in the muted glow of the chandeliers. 'I'm sure I can handle a slow dance,' he said as he rested one hand on her hip and pulled her into his arms. 'Especially if it means I can get my hands on you before midnight,' he whispered against her hair.

She tilted her head back and looked into his handsome face, thrown into stark relief by the shadowy light, suddenly desperate to store up as many memories as she could tonight. In case they were all she had left in the morning.

She clung to him as he swayed her gently in his arms, his limp barely noticeable.

Dropping her cheek onto his shoulder and nestling against the crisp linen of his dress shirt, she listened to the pounding of his heart and revelled in the warmth of his body against hers. The fresh scent of pine soap and the musky scent of male pheromones enveloped her.

So far, despite an extreme case of nerves, the night had been magical—and she didn't want it to end.

The Savoy had been a spectacular venue, done out in its festive finery, the baubles and bows and fairy lights adding a childlike air of expectation to the sedate luxury of the landmark hotel.

The show had been elegant and beautiful and her silk work, which Ruth had incorporated as the signature pieces, had complemented the dramatic setting perfectly. After a standing ovation during her bow on the catwalk, Maddy had sat through the four-course charity dinner afterwards with Rye by her side. And as he'd teased her about the number of people who came up to sing her praises or press business cards into her hand, she'd barely been able to eat a bite.

The thought of what lay ahead, when they returned to the suite Rye had booked for the night, had been hovering at the back of her mind all evening, but it hadn't managed to dim the wonder of being in such a beautiful place with Rye as her attentive escort.

And he had been attentive, playful and charming and ridiculously proud of her achievement. And if she'd noticed the tiniest tension in his tone, the guarded looks he flicked her way when he thought she wasn't looking, she hadn't let it bother her.

Whatever happened tonight, at least she would finally know what he felt for her. Whether what they had was real or imagined. And whether they had any hope at all of making a life together.

As they moved together to the swelling strains of orchestral music, the significance of the moment hit her. She had been a coward, and a foolish one at that, letting her parents' miserable excuse for a marriage stop her from fighting for what she wanted. She'd held back and let Rye take the lead when he knew even less about love than she did.

His arm tightened around her waist as hope and determination made her heart swell to impossible proportions.

Tonight didn't have to be the end. It could be the start of a wonderful new beginning.

'Are you sure? There's a bathroom in the suite,' Rye said, frowning.

'I need a few minutes to freshen up,' Maddy replied, enjoying his frustration maybe more than she should.

'Fine. But hurry up. I feel like I've waited months already.'

Picking up the skirts of her designer gown, Maddy rushed to the Ladies Lounge in the lobby of the grand hotel. Really she could have waited until they got to the suite. But she'd needed a few moments more, to go over in her head exactly what she planned to say to Rye and how she was going to say it.

As she bustled into the ornate cubicle, not paying much attention to the stick-thin woman at the vanity unit who had been one of the models in the show, she realised she wasn't nervous any more. She was excited.

Rye had been so loving tonight, so supportive and so sexy—and the distance, the caution she'd noticed in the last few weeks hadn't been nearly as apparent.

After entering the cubicle, she put the toilet seat down and sat for a moment to collect herself. As excited as she was, she needed to calm down a bit before she went upstairs with Rye. The events of the evening had been overwhelming. She wanted to appear totally sane when she told him she loved him. Babbling would not be good.

As she concentrated on getting her heartbeat back to an acceptable level, she heard the swish of a woman's skirts on the plush carpeting as someone else entered the Lounge.

'Marta, you look fabulous,' the newcomer said in an aris-
tocratic voice. 'How do you manage to stay so thin?'

'Starvation, darling,' the supermodel Maddy had spotted by
the basin said in a wry Germanic accent.

The other woman laughed.

Maddy stood, ready to leave the cubicle.

'I saw your old squeeze Ryan King outside,' the posh
woman remarked. 'No man has a right to look that good in a
tuxedo.'

Maddy's hand stilled on the lock, disconcerted by the news
that the supermodel was yet another of Rye's conquests.

'What were you thinking, letting him get away?' the woman
added. 'He still looks delicious, even with that unfortunate
limp.'

'Looks can be deceiving, darlin',' Marta replied dryly.

The posh woman giggled. 'What does that mean?' she said,
her voice eager with curiosity.

There was a slight pause. Maddy sat back down on the toilet
seat, annoyance catching in her throat. Hadn't Rye suffered
enough without these women gossiping about him as if he were
a piece of meat?

'He's impotent, darlin'. Can't get it up.'

Maddy gasped at Marta's blunt statement, her astonishment masked by another even louder gasp from Marta's
companion.

'You're joking. But he was the most sought-after stud in
London.'

'I know, it's devastating,' Marta replied, not sounding remotely devastated.

'That's so ironic it's almost funny,' the posh woman continued, sounding both scandalised and amused by the juicy titbit
of gossip.

Maddy's stomach clenched, her anger choking her.

How dared these women make fun of Rye's accident? And
they were totally wrong about his abilities in bed. If he'd been
briefly impotent after the accident, he certainly wasn't any
more. She could testify to that.

But, rather than bursting out of the cubicle to set them straight, she found herself anchored to the seat as confusion and inadequacy drowned out her outrage.

A part of her had always wondered why Rye had found her so irresistible. Why he had pursued her. Why he had wanted her so much—a man who could have any woman.

In the weeks since their first few days together, all those silly worries had faded away. Their sex life had been amazing. All his attention, all his eagerness and enthusiasm in bed had bolstered her confidence, not just in her sexual abilities but in so many other areas of her life.

But what if it had all been built on a lie? What if it was her inexperience that had been the real turn-on all along? Had she been his Little Miss Fixit in bed without even realising it?

Was that the real reason he'd become distant in the last few weeks? Because now he was fully recovered he was bored with her?

The thundering in her ears made it impossible to hear the rest of the conversation between Marta and her friend. She felt as if she'd been rooted to the toilet seat for an eternity when she realised she was alone.

Forcing herself to leave the safety of the cubicle, she washed her hands on autopilot, the face that stared back at her in the mirror bleached of colour, all the sweet excitement, all the enthusiastic certainty of a few minutes before sucked out of her.

Rye swore softly as he glanced at his watch for the fiftieth time.

What was she doing? Replumbing all the toilets? She'd been in there over twenty minutes. And, not only that, he'd narrowly avoided bumping into Marta, which would have soured his mood completely.

Shoving his hands into his pockets, he propped his butt against the lobby wall and forced his gaze away from the door of the Ladies Lounge. As he stared at the other guests milling around in the lobby, he tried to swallow down his desperation and a sharp frown creased his brow.

What the hell had happened to his careful plan to back off, to gradually let Maddy go? He'd done all the right things in the last two weeks, even though it had nearly killed him, but he was more desperate to be with her now than ever.

He'd made sure they went out every night since she'd been in London, determined to avoid the intimacy they'd shared in Cornwall.

Several times she'd suggested cooking a meal for him in the penthouse but he'd vetoed the idea, determined not to succumb to the urge to keep her all to himself. If they started living in each other's pockets again, he'd be sunk.

But, every time he deflected her suggestions, he heard the confusion in her voice, saw the hurt in her eyes and it had crucified him.

And, before long, the evenings out had become a major chore. The noise and glamour of London's most exclusive night-spots didn't hold the appeal they once had. And having her with him only made him more aware of how shallow and pointless his old life had really been. He hadn't just missed Maddy. He'd missed the quiet, soothing intimacy of their evenings together in the cottage.

Even so, he'd stuck to his guns—refusing to give in to the weakness.

He'd planned to be politely supportive tonight but not too supportive in case she got the wrong idea. But after she'd gripped his hand during the show, her body vibrating with nerves, his protective instincts had come to the fore. And then when she'd stepped onto the catwalk to take her bow, her face flushed with stunned pleasure, her lush, toned figure in that show-stopping dress making him cross-eyed with lust, he hadn't been able to contain his excitement or his pride a moment longer.

When she'd stepped into his arms on the dance floor and swayed against him to the old-fashioned waltz, he'd found himself holding onto her a bit too tightly. With the weight of her head nestled trustingly on his shoulder, her intoxicating scent making him instantly hard, he was convinced he could have tap danced if she'd wanted him to.

His impatience to get her upstairs, to get her undressed, to claim her in the most basic way possible confirmed what he already knew—and had been desperately trying to deny for weeks. That he didn't just want her any more. He needed her. He depended upon her. In a way he'd promised himself he'd never depend upon anyone again.

He shifted uneasily against the panelled wood, glanced back at the still unmoving door to the Ladies. And felt as if he were teetering on the edge of an abyss.

A cold, black, bottomless abyss which he'd fallen into once before—and which he had vowed never to fall into again.

'Where did all those people come from?' Rye said as he fumbled with the keycard, one hand gripped on Maddy's. 'And why did they all have to pick our lift?' Finally the green light blinked and he hauled her into the suite. 'We must have stopped at every damn floor.'

He pulled her round to face him, pressed her back against the closed door, trapping her body against his and feeling her shudder of response. 'Remind me never to get a suite on the top floor again,' he quipped in a strained voice.

Her eyes were wide and unfocused, her face a little pale, and she'd barely spoken a word since she'd walked out of the Ladies Lounge. But then he hadn't given her much chance, he'd hauled her into the lift so fast.

Bracing his hands against the door, he buried his face against her neck, the erotic scent of her making him harden as she shivered.

'This has been the longest evening of my entire life,' he murmured, the thin leash on his control stretched to breaking point.

He kissed the pulse point on her collarbone, exposed by the off the shoulder gown, skimmed his hand down satin-clad curves, then bent to grasp the hem of her dress. He groaned as he ran questing fingers up the silky skin to the apex of her thighs.

She jumped as he pressed the heel of his palm against the thin silk of her panties, and then writhed as he plunged into velvet heat.

'Please stop, Rye.' She shrank back, her hands flattening against his chest.

He didn't hear the words at first, his heart thundering in his ears, the painful arousal pulsing against his fly. He had to be inside her, had to be seated deep so he could ride them both to orgasm and calm the frantic beats of his pulse.

He moved back to release the straining erection.

'Don't, Rye.' She grabbed his wrist to still his hand on the zip. 'We have to talk.'

He lifted his head, the words registering this time but not making any sense. 'Later.'

But as he bent to kiss her, she twisted away, forcing him to draw back.

'No, now,' she said, her eyes dark with arousal but shadowed with regret. 'We have to talk now.'

Damn, she was serious.

'What's so important we've got to talk about it right this second?' he said, struggling not to snap. Not easy when he had an erection the size of Mount Everest in his pants and panic was skittering up his spine.

She flinched, her emerald eyes widening.

He stepped back, trying to get a chokehold on the need and frustration.

'I want to make love to you, Maddy,' he said, lowering his voice. 'And it's pretty obvious you want to make love to me. So what's this all about?'

She shut her eyes, a sad little sigh issuing from her lips. The dejection in the pose had apprehension twisting in his gut.

'But you wouldn't be making love, would you?' she said, her voice firm but fragile. 'You'd be having sex.'

'What does that mean?' he rasped.

Her eyes opened and he tensed, seeing hurt and accusation.

'I know what you went through,' she said. 'After your accident. That you couldn't perform sexually for a while.'

Horror came first, followed swiftly by denial. 'What?' he croaked.

She straightened, squared her shoulders as if she were gathering her courage. 'You never really cared for me at all, did you? This was always just about the sex.'

He could hear the unhappiness in her voice, see the aching vulnerability in her eyes, and the terrifying abyss widened to an enormous chasm beneath his feet.

Maddy saw him recoil, his face blank with shock before the shutters slammed down.

'What exactly am I supposed to say to that?' he said, his voice hoarse.

'That you *do* care about me?' she said wearily, but the last lingering flicker of hope had already guttered out. He probably did care about her. But it would never be enough. Not if she had to beg him to admit it.

'For God's sake, Maddy, stop being melodramatic. Of course I care about you. Believe me, the sex wouldn't be as good as it is if I didn't.'

She let out a hollow laugh. How could she have been so blind? So foolish? Hadn't she learnt anything from watching her mother go through this same charade throughout her childhood? Debasing herself to get something from her father which he had never been capable of giving her.

'You really don't get it, do you?' she murmured, incredulous at her own stupidity. She blinked furiously, struggling not to let the misery engulf her.

The whole time they'd been together in Cornwall, they'd never even gone out together. All they'd really done was make love in almost every spare minute they had. In the past few weeks, ever since she'd realised how deep her feelings were, she'd deluded herself into believing that those long, lazy, seductive evenings had been a sign of their growing intimacy, their burgeoning love. But they hadn't been. Not for him.

'Don't get what?'

'That I've fallen in love with you, Rye.'

He dropped her arm as if he'd been burned. 'That's insane. Why would you do that?'

Because I thought you needed me. As much as I needed you.

The words burned in her throat but she refused to say them. What would be the point? She'd seen the flash of horror in his eyes at her admission and all the hopes and dreams she'd nurtured so foolishly had finally died.

'I have to go,' she whispered through jerking breaths, her lungs screaming with the effort to hold back the flood of tears.

He'd used her, but she'd let herself be used. And for that she had to take some of the blame.

But, as she turned to leave, he clamped his hand onto her wrist. 'You don't love me, Maddy. You just think you do. You don't even know me.'

She pulled her hand out of his. 'I know you better than you think.' She drew a gulping breath. 'I know you use sex to replace intimacy. I know you refuse to let me get close to you. And I know you'd rather push me away than admit you need me.'

She walked to the door on unsteady legs.

'I'm not pushing you away,' he shouted. 'I want you to stay, damn it.'

Keep breathing. You can get through this.

'Maddy, come back here. Did you hear what I said? I want you to stay.'

She opened the door, refused to look back at him. 'And I want you to love me,' she said. 'But I know you can't.'

Ignoring the angry shout as he tried to follow her, she picked up her skirts and fled.

CHAPTER TWENTY-THREE

MADDY waved the local cabbie off, so exhausted she felt as if her bones were about to melt.

Seeing a dim glow coming from the cottage's living room, she thanked whatever stroke of fate had made her forget to turn off one of the lights when she'd left in such a hurry what felt like a lifetime ago—but had only been sixteen days.

Walking into the empty house now was going to be hard enough; doing it in darkness would probably destroy what little control she had left. She'd spent the night in Cal's spare room in Hampstead, fielding his barrage of questions about what the hell had happened to her and why she had only a ball gown on and no luggage. The ten-hour journey home on two different trains wearing the too-tight sweater dress one of Cal's many girlfriends had left behind hadn't helped to stabilise her mood one bit.

Reaching for the key tucked into the eaves that she left in case of emergency, she resolutely refused to worry about how she was going to get her stuff back from Rye's penthouse. Or how she was going to explain her disappearing act to Ruth. Surely in a couple of days she'd have recovered enough of her composure to contact Ruth and Rye's PA. Contacting Rye wasn't an option. Her lip quivered and she bit into it.

Nearly home. Nearly safe. Don't you dare fall to pieces now. Not when you've managed to keep it together this long.

One thing she'd learned from this whole experience— she was stronger than she had ever imagined. If she could survive this much humiliation and heartache, she could survive anything.

She searched for the key for another few seconds with no luck. Then tried the door out of habit. To her astonishment, it opened.

The fact that she'd been foolish enough to leave her front door unlocked for over a fortnight didn't astonish her for long, though. Wasn't it just another sign of how comprehensively she'd failed herself over the past month?

She shrugged off the coat Cal had lent her in the entrance hall and entered the darkened sitting room.

Her steps halted and fear lanced through her at the sight of the fire flickering in the hearth.

'Hello, Madeleine. You took your time.'

Her head whipped round as her heart punched her ribcage. The ball of agony grew in her chest, pressing against the unshed tears that had been scalding her throat since yesterday.

'What are you doing here?' she whispered, watching as he levered himself out of the armchair.

He looked tall and indomitable, his head skimming the ceiling beams as he made his way towards her, the light from the fire casting his face into shadow. The purpose in his stride wasn't diminished in the least by the slight hitch in his gait.

Panic came first, followed swiftly by shock as he spoke. 'I've come to tell you I love you.' His voice sounded husky, rough with emotion.

But as her heart leapt wildly into her throat, her head registered the truth.

'Don't say that.' She wanted to flee again. But she could barely stand, her legs weak, her knees shaking. And, anyway, where could she flee to? He was in her home, would always be in her heart. This time she had to stand and fight. 'Don't lie to me,' she finished.

She shoved him as hard as she could, but still he stepped forward and took her arm to pull her close. 'I'm not lying.'

Her hands clenched into fists as the tears she'd been fighting back so valiantly coursed down her cheeks. 'I don't believe you.' Her fists pummelled his chest as she hit out to halt the humiliation, to stop the agony.

'Stop it, Maddy.' His voice cracked as he stifled the last of the futile struggle against his chest.

Gulping sobs racked her body. 'Why did it have to be you?' she whispered through jerky sobs, his arms holding her as her body quaked. 'I didn't even believe in love.' The last of the anger drained away to leave only the agony.

'Don't cry.' His voice seemed to come from a million miles away, his hand stroking her hair. For a brief moment she felt comforted and secure, but then reality froze her.

She struggled out of his arms, swiped the tears from her cheeks. 'I want you to leave now.' She'd felt the evidence of his arousal against her belly—and her own traitorous response. 'I know why you're here,' she said, rigidly polite. 'And it won't work. I know you can't love me and I know why. And saying you do won't get me back into your bed, so there's no reason for you to pretend.'

The slashing pain came first, slicing cleanly through the last of Rye's defences. He wanted to grab her, to shake her, to yell at her that he couldn't control his response to her, that he'd never been able to control it. And that he'd been to hell and back in the last twenty-four hours. But he knew every last second of agony he'd suffered had been his own fault, not hers.

The cruel humiliation of seeing her run away from him, his lame leg making it impossible to catch her. The frantic phone calls to discover her whereabouts. The desolation of turning up at the cottage to find the place empty. The knowledge that he'd thrown away the only thing he'd ever needed in his life because of his own cowardice. And now the accusation that he would lie about his feelings for the sake of sex.

Had he really believed that simply telling her he loved her would make up for all the mistakes he'd made? For the way he'd used her and continued to use her and refused even once to confront the truth about how he felt about her?

He deserved her scorn. He deserved her contempt. But,

however guilty he felt, it didn't mean he was going to give up without a fight. He'd been waiting for close to six hours in the cottage, alone, trying to figure out a way to make amends for what he'd done. Everything from kidnap to blackmail to throwing himself on her mercy and hoping for the best had been considered. The only strategy that hadn't was letting her go.

She'd said she loved him. And he was going to hold her to that, no matter what. One huge advantage he had in his favour, and which he clung to now like a life raft in a storm-tossed sea, was that Maddy had more compassion than any person he knew. It was probably why she'd been foolish enough to fall for him in the first place, and he was banking on it being her downfall now.

She'd have to forgive him. Because she was too good a person not to.

'What makes you think I can't love you?' he asked.

Her lip trembled but she held painfully still. Guilt churned in his stomach but he refused to relinquish eye contact, to let her off the hook.

'It's not that you can't; it's that you won't let yourself.'

He nodded. 'And what makes you think that?'

'I don't think that. I know it.' Her shoulders slumped and he noticed the dark smudges under her eyes, the pallor of her skin in the flicker of firelight. He wanted to gather her in his arms, to take her to bed and burn away her distress. But he couldn't take the easy way out. Not again.

He needed to listen to her this time. And then tell her the truth. And hope like hell she still loved him once she realised how wrong she'd been.

He nudged up her chin, brought her gaze to his. 'What do you know, Maddy?'

'That you never recovered from losing your parents. That the loss still haunts you. And that you've never let anyone get close enough to mean that much to you again.'

As she said the words, Maddy saw the flash of raw grief on Rye's face and understood something she'd been trying really hard not to admit. She'd wanted to believe this mess was his fault as well as hers. But was it really? He'd never asked for anything from her except physical pleasure, something he'd given back tenfold. She was the one who had insisted on moving the goalposts—on wanting more from him than he had ever been willing to give. And by not telling him how she felt, by not giving him the chance to set her straight, she'd brought all this misery on herself.

'I'm sorry,' she blurted out. He had never wanted her to fall in love and, as much as he'd manipulated her, he'd never lied to her about that.

He frowned, focused on her. 'Sorry for what?'

She wiped the errant tears off her cheek. 'I tried to make this something it isn't. You never…'

'Don't,' he said, touching a finger to her lips. 'Don't do that.'

'Don't do what?' she said, confused by the curt command.

'Don't make excuses for me.' He ran unsteady fingers through his hair, then swore softly. 'I don't deserve it. If anyone needs to say sorry here, it's me. Not you.' He lifted her hand and pressed his lips into her palm. 'Maddy, it wasn't the loss I couldn't get over. It was the anger at the pointless way they died.'

She tilted her head, hopelessly baffled by the self-loathing in his voice. 'I don't understand.'

He threaded his fingers through hers and held on. 'I should tell you what happened.'

She shook her head. She'd tried to make him relive this once already for her own selfish reasons. She wasn't prepared to do it again. 'You don't have to tell me, Rye. It was never any of my business.'

'Yeah. It is.' He gave a rueful smile, confusing her even more. 'My father had an accident on his board.' He ducked his head but she could hear the tension in his voice. 'It was a World Championship Competition; he wanted to qualify for the top league.' His eyes met hers, the grief so intense it took her breath away. 'She begged him to be careful. But he didn't listen. He took a stupid risk, wiped out against a reef and broke his neck.'

'Rye, please—' she tightened her grip '—don't do this. You don't have to.'

'Yeah, I do.' His Adam's apple bobbed as he swallowed. 'She took an overdose of sleeping pills three weeks later. But really it was like she was already dead. She left me a note. You want to know what it said?'

She flinched at the bitterness in his voice, tears streaming down her cheeks. 'What?'

'Sorry. That's all it said. Sorry. Like that was going to make up for leaving me.'

'Please, Rye. I didn't mean to bring all that...'

'I'm not telling you this to make you feel bad. I'm telling you so you'll understand something. They were selfish people. They loved me, sure. But they always put themselves first. And I've done the same damn thing to you.' He looked at her and the tenderness she saw made her heart stop. 'And it's taken me forever to see it.'

'That's not true,' she said, automatically leaping to his defence. 'You did what you had to do to protect yourself. You were just a little boy.'

'But I'm not a little boy any more,' he said, interrupting her. 'And I haven't been for a long time.' He rested his hands on her hips. 'The truth is, losing them the way I did became a convenient excuse to have everything I wanted without risking anything in return.' He touched his forehead to hers and sighed. 'You want to know what's really ironic?'

She blinked, still baffled, but at the same time oddly elated. The shutters had lifted. She'd never seen Rye so open, had never even thought it was possible.

'Yes, I would,' she said softly.

'Because I kept getting away with it. Because I came out of each relationship unscathed, I always thought I'd be able to choose—who I cared about and how much. And then you came along and suddenly I didn't get to choose.'

Was that gratitude she could see in his eyes or something more?

'I wanted to be with you all the damn time,' he continued. 'And you were right, I wanted to make that all about the sex and nothing else.' A rueful smile tilted his lips. 'But it was never that simple. Was it?'

'Not for me,' Maddy murmured.

'The only difference is,' he added, 'you had the guts to admit it. And I didn't.'

The sensual grin spread, making heat pulse at her core and warmth wrap around her heart. He paused to take a deep breath. 'I do love you, Maddy. In fact, I think I've loved you for weeks. But I was too scared to say it. Even to myself.'

'Oh!' she whispered, pressing her fingers to her lips, tears of emotion pricking the back of her eyes. 'Do you really mean it?' she said, and immediately felt like an idiot.

What was she trying to do—ruin her big romantic moment?

But he didn't look offended or even surprised; his grin just got bigger. 'I do if you do.'

She sprung up on tiptoe and flung her arms around his neck. 'You know I do.'

He chuckled, his arms holding her as she dampened his shirt collar with happy tears.

'I brought a nice bottle of Chablis with me, in the hope that I could persuade you to give me another chance,' he murmured, his hot breath brushing her ear lobe. 'How about I open it?'

She giggled, rejoicing in the feel of him swelling to life against her midriff. 'Only if you promise to drink it naked.'

He laughed, then gripped her tight and lifted her off the ground.

Her delighted peals of mirth mingled with his husky chuckles as he spun her round, then lost his balance and tumbled them both onto the sofa.

The last of their laughter subsided as he brushed her hair back and framed her face. 'I will if you will,' he said, the tender promise shining in his eyes.

'Oh, all right, then,' she whispered, struggling to fake a frown. 'If you insist.'

And, much to her everlasting joy, he did.

EPILOGUE

'ARE you happy, Maddy?'

'Can't you tell, Cal?' Maddy smiled at the sober concern in her brother Callum's smoky green eyes as he held her loosely round the waist to swing her into a turn.

'I'm not just happy. I'm blissfully, overwhelmingly and unbelievably happy.'

Or she would be once she got up the guts to tell Rye the news she'd kept buried inside since this morning.

As her brother danced her round under the bows of holly and mistletoe, the flicker of candlelight and torches illuminating Trewan Manor's stately ballroom, she scanned the large gathering of friends who she and Rye had invited to witness their marriage vows that afternoon. Her heart caught in her throat for what felt like the fiftieth time that day when she caught sight of her new husband of two hours standing beside the dance floor, deep in conversation with his best man Phil and his friend Zack, who had travelled all the way from California with his family the day before.

Rye looked like a pagan Prince Charming, the careless waves of dark blond hair touching his collar, the silk tie he had worn for the ceremony now tucked into the back pocket of his suit trousers and the top buttons of his dress shirt undone to reveal the whorls of chest hair.

The insistent pulse of heat throbbed as she imagined undressing him the rest of the way in a few hours time.

'He almost deserves you,' her brother murmured in her ear.

'So I guess I'll have to live with the fact that he's turned my smart, sensible little sister into a starry-eyed romantic.'

She tore her eyes away from Rye to find Cal studying her in that inscrutable way he had that always reminded her why he was one of the top barristers in the country.

Her cheeks flushed.

'You really are happy, aren't you,' he said, but the familiar cynicism made his irises glint like emeralds.

Maddy's smile faltered, a pang of regret piercing through the daze of euphoria—and unbridled lust. How could she and Cal have grown up witnessing the same misery and become such different people—with such different needs?

Yes, she had once been as suspicious as Cal about the existence of love.

But, despite that, she had always wanted to build a stable, secure relationship that would finally make her forget about the emotional roller coaster of their childhood. And what she'd eventually found with Rye had been so much more than that staid partnership she'd once craved.

What they had together was a miracle as wonderful as it was unexpected. After a year together, the life they shared was still an electrifying ride of passion and excitement, comfort and companionship.

Dividing their time between London and Cornwall and turning the dark empty rooms of Trewan Manor into the home it was always meant to be had given them the best of both worlds—not just the energy of the big city but also the gentler pace of rural life. And every so often, when they felt the need to take a time-out from everything, they'd turn off their mobile phones and lock themselves away in the cottage on the cliff path.

Her silk design work had turned so swiftly from adored pastime to thriving business that her feet had yet to touch the ground. But Rye had been with her every step of the way, offering support and advice and encouragement, and even distraction when necessary. She grinned. The morning before her last show, he'd diligently seduced her into a puddle of lust to take her mind off the worst case of nerves known to woman.

She touched her hand to her midriff as the music slowed to a stop. Tonight, she and Rye would enter a new phase that would bring more daunting challenges. But, however stunned she'd been this morning, she knew they'd be facing this new challenge together.

'Yes, I really am happy, Cal.'

I wish you could be too, she thought wistfully, but didn't say it, knowing Cal would be amused by the sympathy, and appalled by the sentiment. She would give anything for her handsome, commanding and deeply cynical brother to be able to find love—or at least open himself to the possibility. But Cal had built a fortress around himself that she suspected no one would ever be able to penetrate.

'Thank you for giving me away today,' she added, dispelling the foolish ripple of melancholy. 'I know fairy tale weddings aren't your scene.'

Her heart pounded as impatience and anticipation consumed her. She needed to find Rye and tell him her news; she had waited long enough already. But, as she turned to go, Cal held onto her hand.

'Mads, just so we're clear. If the fairy tale ever ends, you know where to find me.'

She blinked back tears, hopelessly touched by the misguided offer. Cal's protective instinct was one of his most infuriating qualities, but it was also one of his most endearing.

'Thanks, Cal, but don't hold your breath.'

She heard his wry chuckle as she rushed off, lifting the skirt of her bias-cut silk bridal gown.

This fairy tale wasn't going to end, because Rye and she wouldn't let it. Not after everything they'd been through to make it work. The enchantment of their Christmas marriage ceremony and the secret inside her had only reaffirmed the fact that today was about facing the future with courage and love and determination. Not doubts or regrets.

* * *

'Damn! Are you sure?' Rye's face went chalk-white and his hands dropped away from Maddy's waist.

Maddy nodded, pushing down the instinctive spurt of panic. He didn't look displeased, just shocked. Which was exactly how she had felt this morning. She had to give him time to adjust.

'When did you find out?' he asked carefully—so carefully she felt her panic start to increase.

'This morning. I should have told you straight away, I know that. But I was reeling and there was all the wedding business. So I put it to one side, until we could discuss it properly.'

Why did her reasoning sound feeble and cowardly all of a sudden?

He dropped into the chair on the balcony, the muted strains of ballroom music from downstairs the only sound, other than the rasp of his breathing.

Maybe she should have said it more carefully, instead of blurting it out as soon as she'd dragged him out here. But, honestly, was there a subtle way to say 'I'm pregnant'?

They'd never talked about having children, had never even considered it. Which was ridiculous, now she thought of it. When you got married, children were the inevitable next step, but somehow the subject had never come up.

Their careers were both important to them and, even though they had been living together for over a year, their relationship was still very much in the first flush of love. They travelled extensively, had no settled base and their sex life was as exhilarating and spontaneous as it had ever been. Bringing a baby into that would be a major step—it would change everything, and not all of it for the better.

She touched her hand to her waist. But what would she do if he said he didn't want their baby, that he wasn't ready? She wasn't even sure that she was ready herself. But, as soon as the little pink *Pregnant* sign had appeared in the window of the home pregnancy test that morning, this child had felt utterly real to her, so much a part of their life and their future. But, as she watched Rye drag an unsteady hand through his hair, it hit her that he might not feel the same connection.

She sat beside him, covered his hand with hers. 'What are you thinking, Rye?'

Please don't shut me out. Not now.

Rye looked up to find Maddy searching his face. The trust and honesty and total conviction in her gaze made his blood pressure soar into the stratosphere.

How could he tell her that he was both ecstatic and yet so terrified he felt physically sick?

Maddy would be an incredible mother—patient, kind, loving, nurturing and completely selfless. But what kind of father was he going to make? What if he failed? What if he failed Maddy and their baby?

He turned his palm up, squeezed her hand but couldn't push the words out past the lump in his throat.

The fact that she had waited all day to tell him fed his paranoia. Did she want this baby? She hadn't said. What if she already knew what he now feared—that he wouldn't be any good at this?

He stared down at their linked fingers. He had made a promise to love this woman and honour her for the rest of his life in the tiny church ten miles down the coast road only this afternoon. But what if that wasn't enough?

'Whatever it is you're thinking, you have to tell me,' she whispered.

Hearing the tremor in her voice, he forced the panic down. He was scaring her.

He'd made another promise a year ago—that he would never lie about his feelings again to Maddy or himself—and he'd been given riches beyond measure as a result. Maddy's smile every morning when he woke up, her silky soft body curled against him every night, the sound of her laughter when he teased her, the tantalising scent of her skin...

He guessed this was the 'for better or worse' the vicar had mentioned earlier. He just hadn't been prepared for 'better' *and* 'worse' to sock him right in the solar plexus at exactly the same time.

He sucked a deep breath of the wintry air into his lungs, blew it out slowly.

Good God, I'm going to be a daddy.

Gripping Maddy's fingers, he turned to her at last. 'Truthfully?' He settled his other hand in her lap, stroked it over the smooth silk covering her belly. 'I'm overwhelmed and totally petrified.'

The quick smile that lit her face had his heart punching his chest. She threw her arms round his shoulders, her laughter calming the frantic beats of his pulse.

'Snap,' she whispered as happy tears dampened his neck.

And, just like that, the fear and uncertainty began to disappear.

He pulled back, held her at arm's length. 'We must be nuts,' he murmured as pride and awe thickened his voice. 'Are we seriously having a baby?'

She nodded, beaming with hope and confidence. 'I will if you will.'

He crushed her to him, the surge of adrenalin, the feeling of rightness reminding him of that pure flawless moment when his surfboard caught the perfect wave.

Only this time the giddy rush of triumph and invincibility was even more intoxicating because he knew it would last for ever—and he wasn't riding the wave alone.

Harlequin Presents

Coming Next Month

from **Harlequin Presents®**. Available April 26, 2011.

Coming Next Month

from **Harlequin Presents® EXTRA**. Available May 10, 2011.

**Visit www.HarlequinInsideRomance.com
for more information on upcoming titles!**

REQUEST YOUR FREE BOOKS!

2 FREE NOVELS PLUS
2 FREE GIFTS!

YES! Please send me 2 FREE Harlequin Presents® novels and my 2 FREE gifts (gifts are worth about $10). After receiving them, if I don't wish to receive any more books, I can return the shipping statement marked "cancel." If I don't cancel, I will receive 6 brand-new novels every month and be billed just $4.05 per book in the U.S. or $4.74 per book in Canada. That's a saving of at least 15% off the cover price! It's quite a bargain! Shipping and handling is just 50¢ per book in the U.S. and 75¢ per book in Canada.* I understand that accepting the 2 free books and gifts places me under no obligation to buy anything. I can always return a shipment and cancel at any time. Even if I never buy another book, the two free books and gifts are mine to keep forever.

106/306 HDN FC55

Name	(PLEASE PRINT)	
Address		Apt. #
City	State/Prov.	Zip/Postal Code

Signature (if under 18, a parent or guardian must sign)

Mail to the **Reader Service**:
IN U.S.A.: P.O. Box 1867, Buffalo, NY 14240-1867
IN CANADA: P.O. Box 609, Fort Erie, Ontario L2A 5X3

Not valid for current subscribers to Harlequin Presents books.

**Are you a current subscriber to Harlequin Presents books
and want to receive the larger-print edition?
Call 1-800-873-8635 or visit www.ReaderService.com.**

* Terms and prices subject to change without notice. Prices do not include applicable taxes. Sales tax applicable in N.Y. Canadian residents will be charged applicable taxes. Offer not valid in Quebec. This offer is limited to one order per household. All orders subject to credit approval. Credit or debit balances in a customer's account(s) may be offset by any other outstanding balance owed by or to the customer. Please allow 4 to 6 weeks for delivery. Offer available while quantities last.

Your Privacy—The Reader Service is committed to protecting your privacy. Our Privacy Policy is available online at www.ReaderService.com or upon request from the Reader Service.

We make a portion of our mailing list available to reputable third parties that offer products we believe may interest you. If you prefer that we not exchange your name with third parties, or if you wish to clarify or modify your communication preferences, please visit us at www.ReaderService.com/consumerschoice or write to us at Reader Service Preference Service, P.O. Box 9062, Buffalo, NY 14269. Include your complete name and address.

With an evil force hell-bent on destruction,
two enemies must unite to find a truth that turns
all-too-personal when passions collide.

Enjoy a sneak peek in Jenna Kernan's next installment
in her original TRACKER *series, GHOST STALKER,*
available in May, only from Harlequin Nocturne.

"**W**ho are you?" he snarled.

Jessie lifted her chin. "Your better."

His smile was cold. "Such arrogance could only come from a Niyanoka."

She nodded. "Why are you here?"

"I don't know." He glanced about her room. "I asked the birds to take me to a healer."

"And they have done so. Is that *all* you asked?"

"No. To lead them away from my friends." His eyes fluttered and she saw them roll over white.

Jessie straightened, preparing to flee, but he roused himself and mastered the momentary weakness. His eyes snapped open, locking on her.

Her heart hammered as she inched back.

"Lead who away?" she whispered, suddenly afraid of the answer.

"The ghosts. Nagi sent them to attack me so I would bring them to her."

The wolf must be deranged because Nagi did not send ghosts to attack living creatures. He captured the evil ones after their death if they refused to walk the Way of Souls, forcing them to face judgment.

"Her? The healer you seek is also female?"

"Michaela. She's Niyanoka, like you. The last Seer of Souls and Nagi wants her dead."

Jessie fell back to her seat on the carpet as the possibility of this ricocheted in her brain. Could it be true?

"Why should I believe you?" But she knew why. His black aura, the part that said he had been touched by death. Only a ghost could do that. But it made no sense.

Why would Nagi hunt one of her people and why would a Skinwalker want to protect her? She had been trained from birth to hate the Skinwalkers, to consider them a threat.

His intent blue eyes pinned her. Jessie felt her mouth go dry as she considered the impossible. Could the trickster be speaking the truth? Great Mystery, what evil was this?

She stared in astonishment. There was only one way to find her answers. But she had never even met a Skinwalker before and so did not even know if they dreamed.

But if he dreamed, she would have her chance to learn the truth.

Look for GHOST STALKER by Jenna Kernan,
available May only from Harlequin Nocturne,
wherever books and ebooks are sold.

HNEXP0511

Harlequin Romance

Don't miss an irresistible new trilogy
from acclaimed author

SUSAN MEIER

IN THE BOARDROOM

Greek Tycoons become devoted dads!

Coming in April 2011
The Baby Project

Whitney Ross is terrified when she becomes guardian
to a tiny baby boy, but everything changes when
she meets dashing Darius Andreas, Greek tycoon
and now a brand-new daddy!

Second Chance Baby (May 2011)
Baby on the Ranch (June 2011)

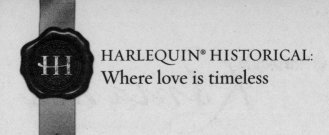

HARLEQUIN® HISTORICAL:
Where love is timeless

Claimed by the Highlander

FROM FAN-FAVOURITE AUTHOR

MICHELLE WILLINGHAM

SCOTLAND, 1305

Warrior Bram MacKinloch returns to the Scottish Highlands to retrieve his bride—and the dowry that will pay for his brother's freedom.

His wayward wife, Nairna MacPherson, hopes for an annulment from her estranged husband who has spent most of their marriage in prison.

But the boy she married years ago has been irrevocably changed by his captivity. His body is scarred, nightmares disturb his sleep, but most alarming of all is *her* overwhelming desire to kiss every inch of his battle-honed body....

Available from Harlequin® Historical
May 2011

Look out for more from the MacKinloch clan coming soon!

A *Romance* FOR EVERY MOOD™

www.eHarlequin.com

HH29642

Love Inspired
HISTORICAL
INSPIRATIONAL HISTORICAL ROMANCE

*Introducing a brand-new
heartwarming Amish miniseries,*

AMISH BRIDES
of Celery Fields

Beginning in May with

Hannah's Journey

by ANNA SCHMIDT

Levi Harmon, a wealthy circus owner, never expected to find
the embodiment of all he wanted in the soft-spoken, plainly
dressed woman. And for the Amish widow Hannah Goodloe,
to love an outsider was to be shunned. The simple pleasures
of family, faith and a place to belong seemed an impossible
dream. Unless Levi unlocked his past and opened his heart
to God's plan.

*Find out if love can conquer all
in HANNAH'S JOURNEY,
available May wherever books are sold.*

www.LoveInspiredBooks.com

LIH82868

Fan favorite author
TINA LEONARD
is back with
an exciting new miniseries.

Six bachelor brothers are given a challenge—
get married, start a big family and whoever does
so first will inherit the famed Rancho Diablo.
Too bad none of these cowboys is marriage material!

Callahan Cowboys:
Catch one if you can!

The Cowboy's Triplets (May 2011)
The Cowboy's Bonus Baby (July 2011)
The Bull Rider's Twins (Sept 2011)
Bonus Callahan Christmas Novella! (Nov 2011)
His Valentine Triplets (Jan 2012)
Cowboy Sam's Quadruplets (March 2012)
A Callahan Wedding (May 2012)

HAR75358